HUSHED
WERE
THE HILLS

HUSHED
WERE
THE HILLS

Millie McWhirter

ABINGDON PRESS
Nashville & New York

HUSHED WERE THE HILLS

Copyright © 1969 by Millie McWhirter

Standard Book Number: 687-18105-4

Library of Congress Catalog Card Number: 69-19741

Portions of this book were developed from stories
published earlier in the following magazines: *Coro-
net, Cosmopolitan, Country Beautiful, Redbook,
The Sign,* and *This Week.*

SET UP, PRINTED, AND BOUND BY THE
PARTHENON PRESS, AT NASHVILLE,
TENNESSEE, UNITED STATES OF AMERICA

*TO PAULINE AND POLLY,
FOR ALL THE HILLS WE CLIMBED...*

1

There was a time, before the county seat began to spread, when a community known as Willow Creek drowsed against the lean hills of middle Tennessee.

The time was the early 1930's, before TVA began generating the mystic powers of the river, before high, thin wires rose humming in the wind, prophesying of things to come. In time, a single harsh glare would dispel the night. Small, square boxes would speak with tongues, and monstrous, inhuman eyes would envision strange happenings.

And yet, though the new magic has manifested itself in curious ways, it still bears a certain kinship to the old magic, long rooted in these hills.

Even during the early 1930's, when I ran barefoot over the warm furrows of earth, the glow of kerosene lamps held the night shadows at bay. Spirited whispers transmitted the news as well as any loud speaker in any small box. And always there was the human eye, the eye of the beholder, to bear witness to everything looming on the horizon of Willow Creek.

Willow Creek was some twelve miles out from the county seat, on the winding dirt road that turned off just this side of the levee.

The turnoff was marked by a weathered sign with an arrow to point the way. But the earth was sandy here, and the old sign leaned back against the blackberry bushes, its arrow pointing down toward the creekbed, as if the traveler should look to it for directions. But the creek just lolled along over the rocks, sucking at the roots of the willow, offering no clue to strangers who might come noseying up this road.

This was a narrow road, more'n likely mired up in winter, covered with high water in early spring. It was only when the days lengthened, when the dust became soft and warm, that the road blossomed out with a white edging of Queen Anne's lace, as if Mother Nature had spent the winter here, crocheting.

But outsiders rarely saw this road, seldom came this way. And if, during the early 30's, some stranger had come into the General Store declaring that one day the highway from Town would be widened, that the route to Willow Creek would be blacktopped, folks would've just leaned back in their split-bottomed chairs and vowed the stranger spoke tomfoolery.

Folks considered this community far removed from the county seat, which was always known as

Town. And though Town was showing some signs of spreading, some slight easing of boundaries, there was still nothing down there that prophesied of what was to come. There were only the tent revivalists trumpeting of fire and brimstone, and the wooden benches around Court Square lettered with the premonition—"Long Funeral Home."

But then came the war years when the smoke of industry began seeping into the county, signaling the growth of factories, the fattening of the land. And so, in time, the highway from Town was widened into six lanes, the weathered sentinel at the junction was replaced by a rigid, metal sign. Nowadays, the dusty road to Willow Creek lies buried under the blacktop.

Nowadays, strangers hear motors droning over the countryside. They see smoke signaling up over the ridge, TV aerials jutting from the roofs of small frame houses. And they take these as signs that things are happening at last in these back hills.

But, in truth, things were happening long ago when there was a hush on these hills, when the long, gray cloud was drifting like a lonesome spirit alongside the ridge, and lightning rods rose up like bony fingers supplicating the heavens.

Things were happening that summer, some thirty years ago, when my mother, my sister Polly, and I first went to live in the hills.

We went during the Depression after my father had died and the bank that held Mother's small savings had closed its doors in bankruptcy. There were no openings in Town for a young teacher whose only teaching experience was the year prior to her marriage. And so, when Mother heard that there was an opening out in the county where the low salary was supplemented by a house to live in, she applied and was accepted.

There were those who warned her that the hills were hard, no place for a young widow with two small girls. Polly was five, and I going on eight. "Why, there's no electricity out there," they said, "no running water! What on earth will you do?"

"Well, I guess I'll just make do," she said. "Isn't that what the hill people say? They make do, and so will we."

And so we went to Willow Creek.

We went out to that wide place in the dusty road where the train always gave a long, lonely whistle as it neared the crossing. Up on the hillside the mules would pause, lifting their ears. Children would run down, preparing to wave, while women stood out on their porches, craning their necks to see if the train would be flagged down.

Usually it wasn't, and it would go grumbling on past the huddle of buildings that were the Post Office, the cotton gin, the General Store. The General Store was the center of activity, the local network through which the news was spread, where a weather report was issued every time the screen door opened.

Just past the store was a stand of cottonwoods, a glimpse of the flagpole yonder in the schoolyard.

The school was originally a one-room building, but recently the county had seen to it that more young'uns got their schooling, so another room was hitched on. Mother was hired to teach fifth through eighth grades, while Miss Wilkins continued to ride herd on the beginners.

There beyond the school was the path that dog-legged in from the road, leading toward the small frame house.

It was a three-room house, built long ago with oak taken from the hills, set on stone cleared from the fields. But now it was old, and it leaned slightly away from its foundation, like a mongrel trying to break its tether, to go sneaking back into the woods.

The house brightened up some that first fall after Mother took over its care. She made cretonne cushions for the wicker chairs that had set solemnly nodding out on the porch, and now when the wind came shuffling through dry leaves those chairs rocked gaily, flaunting their cushions. When school let out for cotton picking, she turned her attention to the porch swing. It had been blistered and peeling 'til it made you itch just to look at it, but then she wire-brushed it, rubbed it down, painted it forest-green.

There was some paint left over, and so on a September afternoon the three of us took the can and walked down the path to the wooden mailbox alongside the road.

Polly was first to dabble green onto the weathered post, and then Mother handed me the small brush from my watercolor set. "And Mildred can print our name," she said.

Carefully, holding my mouth just right, I lettered WASSON on the mailbox. Then we all stood back and squinted at it. We nodded, satisfied. The home place had a name.

That day, we gathered rocks from the ditch and mounded them around that rickety post, trying to make it stand up straight. But always, it was an ornery thing and would slouch down again the moment our backs were turned. The house, too, continued to shift and sigh whenever the wind whistled around the eaves, as if the wind were a relic from better days, brighter seasons.

And yet, we were to see a diversity of days together, that old house and Mother and Polly and me.

We were to see the unfolding of many seasons, not only as they appeared on the ridge, but as they came into the lives of those who lived in Willow Creek. For this was a place, a time, when every season was manifested beneath the high, pitched roofs, as surely as it was on the hills.

There was the loneliness of winter, when the fields

lay barren, and icicles weighted the willow with frozen tears.

There was the joy of spring, when the creek rose singing in its bed, while the warm moist earth embraced the farmer's plow, nurtured his seed.

Sometimes, the summer brought in a benevolent sun to swell the crop, gentle rains to issue forth a harvest that filled the corn cribs.

But sometimes, the sun just glared down from a hot, cloudless sky, while the fields produced only dust devils to cavort across the furrows, dancing like death toward autumn.

And yet the hill people did have a way of making do, of biding their time, knowing that no season lasts forever.

"When you've about reached the end of your rope," they said, "you tie a knot. You hang on. You look to the hills."

This, then, is the story of those hills, and the people who lived among them.

This is what they looked for.

This is what they saw.

2

As each season arrived in Willow Creek it brought in specialties for the table, like women carrying covered dishes to a church meeting.

First came the New Year with dried black-eyed peas and hog jowl, followed by spring chicken and green apple pie. Soon there'd be okra, sweet corn, and, later, ripe watermelon cooling in the creek. The first cold snap brought in fresh pork and crackling bread, fried rabbit with hominy. Then it was time for possum and sweet potatoes, and back to dried peas.

But during that first year we lived in the hills, it appeared that November would hold little for Mother and Polly and me. That was the moment when Mother turned over the calendar that hung behind our coal-oil stove, and there was the picture of the traditional Thanksgiving dinner.

There was the long, wooden table with a golden brown turkey rising from the platter. There was the large family seated in high-backed chairs, their hands folded, heads bowed, as they waited for the sandy-haired man at the head of the table to give thanks.

As I stood there in the kitchen looking at the picture of that turkey, my mouth began to water. Then I gazed at the faces of those people with such a large family, so much to be thankful for, and my eyes watered too.

My father had been a sandy-haired man, a big, strapping man who hadn't carried insurance because, obviously, "nothing would happen" to him. But something had happened, and now there were only Mother and Polly and me, alone there in the woods.

When Thanksgiving Day came, there'd be just the three of us seated there in the kitchen at the small, round table, and there'd be no strong man to give thanks. There'd be no platter of golden brown turkey either.

Some terrible ailment had hit the turkeys that fall, and the farmers who'd managed to save a few birds were taking them to Town where prices were dear.

But then, early one morning, we saw Mr. Pope's wagon coming down the road, turning in toward our house.

The Popes lived in that gabled farmhouse up past the store. Theirs was a large family with many mouths to feed, but Miz Pope was a plump mother-hen of a woman who frequently sent "The Mister," as she called her husband, with something to help out the teacher.

This particular morning, Polly and I were standing on the porch watching him come. And then, over the rumbling of the wagon, we heard the wild chorus of turkeys hollering from their wooden crates.

The Mister halted the mule, called down to us. "Run tell your Ma I've brought her something."

As Polly ran inside, calling to Mother, I moved nearer the wagon, peering into the crates at the wonderful fat turkeys. Then I heard a wild squawking and saw The Mister wrestling with something beneath the seat of his wagon. Finally, he pulled out a turkey, its wings beating frantically, its wattle shaking out great squawks of complaint.

The turkey had a pink tassel flopping across its nose like a bandage that had come unloosened, and there was a frayed rope tied around one skinny leg. He leaped to the ground just as Mother and Polly came out of the house.

Mr. Pope leaned down and handed Mother the end of the rope. "He's kind of poorly, ma'am," he said, "but the Missus thought you might get some fat onto him 'fore Thanksgiving."

For a moment, we all just stood there looking at the bird.

He was, indeed, a poorly looking bird, with long, bony feet and a scrawny neck. He stood humped over, shaking his wattle, muttering to himself as he pecked at the rope around his leg. Then he lifted his head, blinked those pale eyes at Mother.

Mother smiled up at Mr. Pope. "Why, he looks

just wonderful!" she said. "And the girls and I will certainly enjoy . . ."

I started toward the bird, holding out my hand, saying, "Here boy . . . here . . ."

He ruffled his feathers and let out a loud squawk, daring me to come closer.

"He's kind of ornery, too," The Mister said. "I wouldn't get too close to 'im." He climbed down, shooed the turkey around back of the house, and tied him to a stump. "You'd better keep him tied up, too, so's he don't go wandering off."

And then, giving us a tin can full of feed, he got back in his wagon and started off toward the ridge.

The turkey craned his neck, watching the wagon as it pulled away. Finally he just stood there, blinking his pale eyes, as the rest of the turkeys called back to him.

I tried to make a clucking sound, held out the can of feed. "Here boy . . . here . . ."

He took a step toward me, but his big feet caught in the rope, and he stumbled and fell, beating up a cloud of dust with his wings.

I knew just how he felt. My feet, too, were too long for my skinny legs, and I was always stumbling and falling and feeling embarrassed.

I walked nearer the stump, untangled the rope, and he got up, smoothing his feathers, muttering to himself.

Polly said, "Mil, what'll we name 'im?"

Mother widened her eyes. "Now, girls, you don't *name* turkeys. You just fatten them up and eat them."

"But we won't eat 'im for two weeks," I said. "In the meantime, we have to call him something." I thought a minute. "Rufus," I said. "Rufus Wasson. That's a good name."

We all looked at the turkey.

He lifted his head, blinked his eyes. But he didn't complain. And so Rufus it was.

That very day we started in to get Rufus fattened up. We put some feed in the cracked saucer Mother brought from the kitchen, and we filled a fruit jar with water and turned it upside down in a bowl.

But Rufus acted as if he hadn't the least notion of trying to gain weight. He would peck around in the yard, nibble on whatever he could find in the weeds, but when it came to eating something that would stick to his ribs, he shook his tassel over his nose and turned away. For two days he just wandered around on his big, bony feet, going as far as the rope would allow, and then he'd sit and stare off toward the ridge until it was time to go to roost on the stump.

On the third day I went outside after our mid-day dinner, since it was Polly's turn to help Mother and mine to fed Rufus.

I put his feed in his saucer, and then I turned over an apple crate and sat there beneath the kitchen window trying to coax him.

He pecked a little at his dish and finally ambled nearer to where I was sitting. He looked up at me.

I was sitting there finishing a corn muffin with jam, and, seeing that Rufus seemed interested in it, I put it down on the dry leaves. He stuck his beak in to sample it. He flipped it over, tumbled the jam into the dirt. Suddenly, he gulped down every last crumb of muffin.

I went running back into the house. "Mother, Rufus likes cornbread!" I shouted, happy that I'd discovered a way to fatten him up. "Rufus wants another muffin!"

Luckily, we had one left over, and so I took it out to him. He bobbed his head, clucked, and took quick, deep pecks into the warm cornbread.

The next night at supper I pushed my own muffin aside. "I'll save this for Rufus," I said.

Mother looked at me. "No," she said. "You need to be fattened up yourself. You eat your muffin and I'll make some extra for . . . for our Thanksgiving turkey."

And so in the days that followed Mother made cornbread muffins for Rufus. He'd stand there clucking, his head turned to one side, as we put them down for him, and now he didn't ruffle his feathers when we edged up closer to him. But he kept worrying at that rope around his leg until one morning Mother said, "I think we can untie the turkey now. I don't believe he'll wander off very far."

And sure enough he didn't. He pecked around in the weeds during the day, roosted on a low branch of the tree at night, and he left the yard only to follow Polly and me whenever we walked across the field to the sand ditch, looking for arrowheads.

It was a week before Thanksgiving before we actually talked about how to kill our turkey.

We were sitting at the kitchen table eating supper, when Polly said, "Mother, how do you . . . how d'you kill a turkey?"

Mother hesitated, her fork halfway to her mouth. "Well . . . ," she said. She took a deep breath. "I've seen people wring the heads off chickens, but . . . but, well that turkey's a lot bigger than a chicken." She picked up her glass, set it back down again. "I-I guess the best thing would be just to hold his head down on that apple crate and just . . . ," she grabbed her glass, gulped some water, "just chop it off!"

We stared down at our plates. "Maybe . . . ," I said, "maybe you could ask The Mister to do it. Maybe he'd know a better . . ."

But Mother shook her head. "No," she said, for she was trying to be both mother and father to us. "I'm sure I can manage just fine, just fine."

We sat there for a moment, saying nothing.

Suddenly, we heard a tapping at the window. We looked up, and there was Rufus standing on the apple crate outside the kitchen window. The crate was high enough that Rufus could just see over the window sill, and now he craned his neck, pecking against the glass.

"He must be hungry," I said. "I guess I'd better go take him his cornbread."

But somehow it made my stomach hurt. I watched Rufus gobbling up the bread and wished I hadn't tried so hard to fatten him up. Perhaps if I hadn't fed him so much, we would've had to wait and have him for Christmas dinner.

And yet, whenever I looked at the calendar that hung behind the coal-oil stove, whenever I looked at the picture of that large family and that golden brown turkey, I knew I should be happy that the Popes had given us something so special for our Thanksgiving dinner. For now we would be like other children, like the children in that picture, our hands folded, heads bowed, giving thanks for what we had.

And though my throat hurt whenever I looked at Rufus, there came a day when I knew we just had to have our turkey for Thanksgiving. That was the day we got a letter from Uncle Marvin Love, saying that he'd be coming to share Thanksgiving dinner with us.

Uncle Marvin worked for the railroad in Town, but now he wrote that he was coming out to see to some repairs being done at the crossing. So he'd be able to stay overnight with us and leave late Thanksgiving Day. It was a wonderful surprise, and now the day was going to be just right, just like the picture. There'd be a man, Mother's brother, there at the head of the table, giving thanks for our golden brown turkey.

When Mother read the letter, she sank down in the rocker and let out her breath. "And *Marvin* will know how to kill the turkey," she said.

It was true that Uncle Marvin could do most anything. He'd been "with the road" for years, had traveled as far as El Paso, Texas, working with the crews, and he could tell stories that'd make your skin prickle. But more than that, he had a talent he'd inherited from his father, a Methodist circuit rider. He could sit down at the table, lift his eyes, and intone a blessing with such feeling you'd think the Lord was up on the roof, listening. Yes, Uncle Marvin would be exactly right to complete the picture of a bountiful Thanksgiving.

And so, as the day approached, I tried to think only of the fact that Uncle Marvin would be with us for Thanksgiving. I tried not to think that Rufus wouldn't be. Or that he would be, but . . .

Uncle Marvin's train was due late in the afternoon. That day, I had made our centerpiece of nuts and gourds, and now Polly was helping Mother cut strips for the mincemeat pie. I was privileged to go to the crossing and meet the train.

Now as we heard the long, lonely whistle echo

through the hills, I grabbed my coat, tied Rufus up so he wouldn't follow me, and ran across the fields.

As the train slowed, Uncle Marvin swung down from the steps. He was a black-haired, wiry man, with strong arms to hug me to his chest. He had brought a sack of red apples, and as we started back toward the house, he rubbed one against his sleeve and handed it to me.

"And what shall we give thanks for tomorrow?" he said.

This was his Sunday voice now, and I wanted to give the right answers.

"Well," I began, "we're thankful that you're here."

He smiled. "Ah, yes . . . but I can't be here every day. There must be something more than that, something you're thankful for every single day."

I swallowed hard, my apple sticking in my throat. We had the turkey, of course, but only for a day, too. And we didn't have much, Mother and Polly and me.

I scuffed my feet in the dust, wishing Uncle Marvin wouldn't force me, afraid I might cry, for I thought as a child thinks, more of tangible things that one could hold or wear or show the other kids at school.

Uncle Marvin was quiet a moment, too. He was not able to give us much that was tangible, for he had a large family in Town, and this was the time of Depression.

"Well," he said finally, "you don't have measles, do you?"

I shook my head. "I had that when we lived in Town, remember?"

"And how about the whooping cough?"

He knew, well as I did, that both Polly and I caught whooping cough just after school started when we first came here. Mother had spent many days running back and forth from the house to the school, many nights holding a basin as we whooped and strangled and tried to swallow coal oil and sugar, the accepted remedy here in the hills.

Uncle Marvin put his hand on my head, tugging gently at my braids. "You see?" he smiled. "There are many things you don't have. Be thankful for that."

We were nearing the path now, and Mother and Polly ran out onto the porch, waving to us.

Uncle Marvin rushed up the step, swung Polly into the air, and then as we went inside he set the bag of apples on the table, started to remove his coat.

"Marvin, before you take off your coat," Mother said, "would you . . . well, I've been waiting for you to . . . would you go kill our Thanksgiving turkey?"

She reached for the ax which was there beside the wood box. She gripped it so hard her knuckles were white, the veins standing out on her hands. "He-he's right outside the window there."

Suddenly, my heart stopped, and yet the blood

24

kept pounding in my ears. "But . . . but . . . ," I began, "c-couldn't you w-wait 'til after supper?"

Mother looked at Uncle Marvin, and a look of understanding passed between them. "Please," she said to him. "Please do it quickly."

Rufus was sitting outside there on the apple crate, looking in the window.

Polly put her hands over her face. Her shoulders were heaving.

Suddenly, tears gushed from my eyes, and I began to sob, painful, racking sobs beyond control.

Uncle Marvin leaned the ax handle against the stove. "Well I reckon there's no hurry," he said. "It's nothing that can't wait 'til after supper."

And so, with this sudden reprieve, my sobs slowed to a sniffle. Polly took her hands down from her face, wiped her nose with her sleeve, and we began setting the table for supper.

At supper, Uncle Marvin told funny stories, rolling his eyes, wrinkling his nose till we couldn't help but laugh. Later, we sat by the fire roasting chestnuts while Uncle Marvin whittled on a piece of kindling and told tales about his years "with the road." Finally, as the fire's embers shifted slow and warm, our eyes were closing, and Polly and I didn't resist when Mother led us into the other room and tucked us into bed.

But it was a restless sleep. I kept waking up, thinking I heard a turkey gobbling. I felt Polly tossing beside me, and once I whispered, "Polly . . . Polly . . ." But she lay very still, not answering.

When I woke again, the room was pale with the early light, and I smelled coffee perking. I threw back the quilts, ran across the cold linoleum into the kitchen.

Mother was sitting there at the table, stirring cream into her coffee. At Uncle Marvin's place was his used cup, stacked on his cleaned plate. He was nowhere in sight. I took a deep breath and walked ever so slowly to the kitchen window. I looked out.

Rufus was there. His head was firmly on his neck. His tassel was hanging jauntily over his nose as he pecked around in the weeds.

And then I saw Uncle Marvin coming out of the woods, crossing the field. His breath was a thin, white stream of whistling, and he was swinging a small willow snare in one hand. In the other, he swung a fat, grey rabbit.

I ran, shouting, back to the bedroom. "Wake up, Polly!" I cried. "Wake up! We're having fried rabbit for Thanksgiving dinner!"

She jumped out of bed and we hollered and laughed and leaped around on the cold floor.

And it was a wonderful Thanksgiving dinner.

Mother baked the chestnut and cornbread dressing in a skillet, with cracklings to flavor it. She spread her lace tablecloth on the kitchen table and centered it with the nuts and gourds and red apples. There was a dish of candied sweet potatoes, a bowl of green beans, a platter of golden brown rabbit.

We took our places at the table, folded our hands, bowed our heads just like in the picture. Uncle Marvin lifted his eyes and began to speak.

"Lord," he began, "we give thanks on this day for Thy many blessings . . ."

As he hesitated, ready to count them one by one, there came a tapping at the window. I turned my head ever so slightly and peeked toward the glass.

There was Rufus, standing outside on the apple crate, tapping on the frosted windowpane.

Uncle Marvin was silent. I saw now that he was peeking, too. So were Mother and Polly.

Uncle Marvin grinned, raised his glance to ours and then on up toward the ceiling. "And O Lord," he intoned, "we're mighty thankful for that which we *don't* have, too. Amen!"

Then, as he began serving up the rabbit, Mother got a saucer, heaped it with cornbread dressing, and I carried it out and served it to Rufus there beside the window. I went back to our family, and as we sat at the table enjoying our Thanksgiving dinner, Rufus sat on the apple crate, enjoying his.

And we were thankful. All of us.

3

The old McFarland place was vacant at the time we first went to Willow Creek. It stood at the end of a rutted lane, up a rise where the giant willow caught every breath of air stirring in these hills.

But little else was stirring up there.

Whenever folks reached that spot where the lane curved up from the road, they hustled past, averting their eyes, not daring to meet the hollow-eyed stare of that house, not wanting to hear the whispering of that willow. And yet, simply by standing there, the old place bore witness to the strange thing that had come down on the McFarlands.

The last of those McFarlands had taken off just last winter, and no one had seen hide nor hair of 'em since. So the talk was dying down, and it seemed that the women would find themselves with no alternative but to close the lid on the whole affair.

But then Mother and Polly and I came to the hills, and the women discovered a brand new audience for the story.

They came calling on the new teacher, bringing muscadine jelly, dressed catfish, a mess of pole beans. And then they brought up the story of the McFarlands, laid it out for the viewing.

The women seemed always to follow a kind of ritual before they began the story.

They'd stand on the porch just passing the time of day, until they turned toward the step, like they were aiming to leave. Then they'd glance out past the creek, squint up toward the rise where you could just make out the dark roof of the old McFarland place.

"See that giant tree moving up yonder?" they'd say, pointing, sometimes taking your arm to move you to a vantage spot. "See how it's stroking the eaves? That's what done it all!"

They'd ease themselves into the wicker chair and begin a steady rocking, jogging their memories for every detail.

" 'Course, they ought to've known better," they'd say. "Those folks was warned against lettin' a willow grow up alongside the house. But then they weren't born to these hills, y'know. They was from off."

The rocker would slow for a moment as they closed their eyes. In hushed voices they began again. "He who dwells beneath the willow," they vowed, "will have cause to weep."

Now with the story begun, the words came faster

as they told about Isabel McFarland, the pretty red-haired one, and about Wade Sanders, who still bore the mark of his love for her.

Isabel, they said, went away last November, vowing never to return. And now it was summer, and she'd not been seen again in these parts. "Lord willin'," they said, "we'll never lay eyes on another McFarland for the rest of our natural days."

And yet, even as they spoke of Isabel, they seemed to see her, plain as day, in the mind's eye. And they brought in her image so clearly that we, too, got a good look at her, even before the day came when we actually saw her in the flesh. We knew why she and her pa had come to Willow Creek in the first place and why there was cause for weeping from the moment they moved into that old house, furnishing it with a few old pieces their kinfolks had left long ago in the barn.

Isabel and her pa had moved into that house just a year ago this coming September, and they were routed from these hills this past winter. So it was plain that their stay was doomed from the day it began.

That particular day had been witnessed by several of the women who told us about it. And now, with total recall, they brought in the sight, the sound of it.

Mother would sit there in the swing, frowning a bit. Sometimes she'd try to interrupt the weird tale with a "But . . ."

But Polly and I sat on the worn, wooden step, our arms clasped over our knees, taking it all in.

The day they recalled began on a morning last September, when the earth was dry and feverish, and folks had gone early to the store 'fore the heat of the day set in. They were clustering around, waitin' on Miss Ada to fill their orders, when Mrs. Pierson came hustling in, wide-eyed, breathless.

The Piersons lived around the bend from the old McFarland place, but the woods thinned out there, giving them a view. Last night, Mrs. Pierson vowed, she'd heard a flatbed truck rattling up that rutted lane. Then she could make out a lamp moving like a ghost inside that deserted house. She'd watched from her window 'til the moon was high, and she finally spied the truck, empty now, she could tell from the sound of it, disappearing down the road.

Well, it was a curiosity, to say the least.

That old place had been deserted for years. Only the willow remained, swaying and sighing over that house like a paid mourner. Certainly no one else grieved over the McFarlands being gone.

Those McFarlands had been peculiar folks right from the start. They'd come here from off, all high and mighty, aiming to get rich from lumbering. They cut and hauled trees like you'd harvest corn. They built that house on the rise, dug a willow from the creekbed and planted it alongside. Folks here warned 'em never to plant a willow where it'd stroke the roof. But they paid no mind. Not 'til their lumber business failed, and the land—all pockmarked now —was wasting away. Then they cursed their luck and left these hills, leaving those pockmarks to cause a regular plague 'round here. Even now, farmers struggled to keep their soil from washing clean off to Georgia.

In time, the next of kin took over the place, took to dairying. He grinned when folks warned him 'bout the willow. But, ha!, he wept when the scour came on his cattle and spread through the hills. That was a hard year for everything 'cept buzzards.

That was several years ago, and the house had stood empty for some time.

But now Mrs. Pierson had witnessed a light moving around the old place. "It's like an apparition," she said, "sure as the world."

"Naw," a farmer said. "It's one of them McFarlands."

And folks were hard put to know which was worse.

Even as they stood there in the store wondering on it, the screen door creaked open.

The morning sun cast the long shadow of a man across the pine floor.

He was a gaunt man with a red mustache, with hair going gray at the temples. He wore a hard straw hat with a wide band. His wash pants were belted.

There was a dead silence while folks eyed the

man and then looked toward Miss Ada Sanders who was standing there behind the counter.

The Sanders owned the store as well as the gin, but Miss Ada's husband was given to back trouble during the busy season. So it was Miss Ada who wore the white store apron. It was their son Wade who kept the boiler going at the gin.

Now Miss Ada tightened her sash, looked straight at the stranger.

"The name's McFarland," he said. "Lester McFarland."

Miss Ada looked up toward the buckets swinging from the rafters. "Saints preserve us," she said.

Whenever the women repeated what Miss Ada had said that day, Mother would nod, knowing they spoke true. This is exactly what Miss Ada would've said. Miss Ada was always looking up at the rafters, calling for the Saints to preserve her. And, apparently, they had.

She was a tall, wiry woman, married some thirty years to Mr. Buford. But everyone, including her husband, still called her Miss Ada.

She was also Wade's mother, but this only gave credence to the saying that babies are found in the cabbage patch. It seemed unlikely that Miss Ada would've gotten a baby any other way.

Now Miss Ada was first to speak. "You come wantin' credit?" she said, narrowing her eyes, giving him the answer even as she put the question to 'im.

Miss Ada's books still showed debts from those first McFarlands. She still mourned Hazel, her good jersey taken by the scour. Her only son's birthright was gnawed with gullies. So it's no wonder she was looking hard at Lester McFarland.

He sidestepped the question. "We're from Ohio," he said, "me and my daughter Isabel. My cousin deeded me that old house down the road."

"You aimin' to farm?"

He shook his head. "It's just a roof over our heads 'til the factory opens back up. We're just trying to last out the Depression, me and my motherless child."

Well, you could hear folks let out their breaths. If this McFarland only aimed to stay for a spell, he mightn't stir up much trouble. So the men motioned McFarland to sit while they edged up their chairs and listened to him tell how the Depression had struck those big factories up North. They even smiled a little at his speech—why, the way he rolled his r's was a real curiosity!

He talked on while the sun rose over the ridge, swung high into the sky. And it was then that the McFarland girl was seen coming down the road, nearing the store.

She looked thinner than a woman ought to, but her green cotton dress swung against the slight curves of her body, and her red hair was bright as sunshine.

She paused at the bottom of the steps. Now you could see that her nose was dusted with gold

freckles, and that lines were etched across her forehead like she had a worried mind. She smiled up at
the solemn faces of folks sitting now on the porch,
but she didn't speak 'til she came up to her pa,
leaned over him. "Dad, you didn't . . ."

He put up his hand, silencing her. He reached into
his pocket, handed her some coins.

She patted his shoulder gently like he was the
young one, and she the old. She went inside the
store, put the money on the counter. "I need some
supplies," she said, soft-like, "much as this'll buy."

Miss Ada glanced at the girl, then at the money.
Miss Ada prided herself on sizing up folks. "Why,
that'll buy a right smart," she said, nice as you please.

But even as she weighed up the sugar, giving extra
measure into the sack, Wade Sanders was leaving
the gin, coming across toward the store.

He passed McFarland there on the porch with
hardly a glance. He was always a serious kind, a hard
worker, and he'd left the gin only to come over for a
cool bottle of Dr. Pepper. Then he opened the screen
door.

The girl was standing there at the counter, her
back to him. She was looking down at her feet, kind
of embarrassed. Her hands were pushed deep into the
pockets of her skirt. But her hair was blowing in the
hot breeze from the fan, and her skirt clung to her
little round behind.

Wade stopped, blinking into the dim light of the

store. And, strange to tell, the girl suddenly turned, looked up at him as if he'd called her name.

Wade drew in his breath. His blue shirt, damp with sweat, tightened over the muscles of his shoulders as he and the girl stood just looking, looking, into each other's eyes.

Well, Miss Ada's mouth turned white. She slapped a side of bacon onto the counter, shoved the brown bags across to Isabel. "*This* oughta' do you," she said.

"Oh," the girl said, turning back toward the counter. "Oh, yes . . . yes, thank you."

McFarland was coming in now taking up the load of supplies. Then he and Isabel left the store, started back toward that old house beneath the willow.

Wade stood at the screen door, watching 'til the girl disappeared 'round the bend of the road, while Miss Ada tightened her apron, yanking at the bow 'til it stood out like wings on a dragonfly.

"But this was the last time," the women said to Mother. "This was the only time when Wade just stood a-watchin'."

It wasn't long 'til Wade took to going up to that old place. It wasn't long, either, 'fore Lester McFarland did what the girl must've feared that first day. He discovered the path that wound back into the hills where he could buy moonshine. But the more he partook of the oh-be-joyful, the less joyful he became.

He'd come down to the store, ease himself into a chair, and sigh that there was still no word of the factory opening up, that he'd come here too late to make a crop, and he could see dark days ahead.

Folks nodded, feeling a chill come on 'em. They knew that the roots of that willow were deep in the earth now and even advising him to cut it down would do not good. Another would just rise up where that one fell. So men began warning McFarland he'd best leave these parts. But he only sat sighing 'til Miss Ada would come out on the porch, shaking her apron at him. "Get along with you," she'd say. "I don't hold with folks talkin' po-mouth!"

But folks allowed it wasn't his talk bothered Miss Ada. It was his daughter Isabel.

Soon you'd see the girl coming down the road just as she had that first day. It was October now, and work was slackening at the gin. So Wade would be watching for the girl, and he'd come walking across to the store, reaching the steps just as she did.

Silently, he'd touch her hand. Together, they'd mount those steps. Then Isabel would pick up her pa's hat there on the floor, straighten it on his head, while she and Wade got on either side of him, steadying him as they walked him on back around the bend.

Well, men took to cornering McFarland, telling him he'd best put a stop to this. "Miss Ada's son is her prize crop," they told him, "and she'll not allow any McFarland to put a blight on his life."

But already, Wade's face was marked with worry. And there was a bruise on his cheek from the day he'd fought the moonshiners back in the hills, trying to make 'em quit selling to Isabel's pa.

So it was that during that fall a year ago now, folks sidled past the old McFarland place, trying not to hear the whispering up there on the rise. But trouble was a-comin', sure as the wind blows.

Then it was November, and winter was settin' in, whitening the hills with hoarfrost, miring the road with freezing rain. That's what caused Miss Ada not to have taken her deposits to the bank in Town, though the metal cashbox was heavy. Many folks were witness to that.

But there was only one witness when the store was broken into, when the cashbox was taken. Only one witness. Miss Ada.

It happened just at dusk, she testified later in County Court. The store had emptied out, and she was closing up when she felt a chill on her neck and realized the back door had come open. Suddenly, a gunnysack was thrown over her head, tightened around her neck. But through the coarse fabric she saw him—McFarland—grab the cashbox and run from the store.

McFarland denied it, raving and ranting to the Judge. "I was warned that woman'd find a way to get rid of us McFarlands," he said. "Folks even warned me that the old place always brought bad

luck to every McFarland. But I never believed it
... 'til now."

Now *his* bad luck was that no one could testify to
his whereabouts at the time of the robbery. He'd
taken the long way home that afternoon, he testified,
'cause the creek was running high, and he feared it
might be over the road. He'd had to circle around his
land, climb the fence, come up past the barn.
When he finally reached his house, he found the
Sheriff there waitin' on him and his poor daughter
crying.

Isabel cried in court, too. Truly, she was a pitiful
sight, pleading with Miss Ada to drop the charges.
"It's all *my* fault," she said, "for letting Wade get
involved with us. But just hate *me* for that. Lock
me up."

But Miss Ada wouldn't back down. "He's a rascal,"
she said.

The Sheriff admitted he'd not found the cashbox,
though he'd searched for it. But he knew Miss Ada
to be a woman of her word, and, if she said McFarland took it, he took it.

So McFarland was taken to the county work farm,
and Isabel got a job in Town, so she'd be near
enough to visit her pa. In a sense, she locked herself
away from Wade, refused ever to see him. She even
returned his letters unopened.

But, just like always, the trouble that came on the
McFarlands was visited on others in Willow Creek.

Now folks began arguing among themselves as to

whether Miss Ada had spoken true, or whether she'd simply seen her chance to rout the McFarlands. It could be that the real thief was still free, walking this very road.

It got so that folks would cut their eyes around at anyone who came into the store with cash in his pocket. Now, as suspicion grew, there was less business, less talking, no joking. Nothing.

But after the loneliness of winter, there came the spring, and as the earth warmed up so did the people. They talked now of planting and the *Farmers' Almanac*. It seemed that the lid was closing on that whole terrible trouble with the McFarlands.

Then, early in September, the afternoon train came slowing along the tracks that passed behind the store. It grumbled to a stop.

We'd gone to the store that day, Mother and Polly and I, to buy Mason jars. School was out now for cotton picking, and Mother was using the time for canning.

Suddenly, those jars began jiggling around on the counter. The train whistled down the valley. Polly and I ran to the back door, pulling at the knob, planning to run out and wave. But ever since last winter, Miss Ada was careful to lock that door long before shadows slipped over the ridge. So now we stood pressing our faces against the glass as the engine went hissing by.

Then the train was slowing to a stop. The conductor jumped down, set out a metal step stool, a suitcase. A pretty red-haired girl stepped down.

The train pulled away, leaving the girl to flounder in its wake. The bawdy wind was lifting her skirt, tousling her hair. She stood with her head bent against the wind, her eyes closed against the cinders. Then she straightened and looked across toward the store.

Folks had shuffled up to the back window, craning their necks to see what was going on. Miss Ada was still standing behind the counter, but as she saw folks looking out at the train and back suddenly toward her, she knew. She marched up to the back door and looked out at the girl standing alongside the tracks.

The girl was wearing a green dress with a red fox fur draped around her shoulders. The fox was the same tawny color as her hair, and with its tail twitching in the wind, its glassy eyes taking on the bright red of the late sun, it was like a vixen guarding her pup.

Miss Ada drew in her breath. "Saints preserve us," she said. She turned, marched back to the counter, began again counting out the Mason jars for Mother, as if she could take up where she'd left off. Ignoring the glances of others there in the store, she looked at Mother. "That girl is Isabel McFarland," she said. "Around here, we give 'er a wide berth."

Mother didn't answer. Her idea of giving someone a wide berth was to offer them a place to sleep. But though she'd told Polly and me that she felt the story was exaggerated, that the hill people tended to have strange superstitions, she knew better than to say that to them.

Now we heard the sounds of heels coming around to the front steps, up across the porch, and the screen door opening. As Isabel stepped inside, her suitcase was banging against her legs, making her walk unsteady.

No one moved or spoke as they eyed the girl. The fox fur made her look like rich city-folk who put on fancy fall clothes even while the weather's still hot. And yet, her green dress showed a faint line where the hem was let down. One of her stockings had a run.

It was Miss Ada who spoke. "You've come back."

Isabel spoke very slowly, like she'd rehearsed. "I've only come for supplies," she said, opening her purse, showing she could pay. "I'm only here to tidy up the house for my father." She hesitated. "He's coming back. He gets out next week, you know, Miss Ada. He says he learned about farming out ... out at that ... that place, and he plans ..."

Miss Ada narrowed her eyes. "He plans to start digging, is that it? And what's he aimin' to dig for?"

Isabel bit her lip, looked down at her feet. The fox slipped off her thin shoulder.

It was then the screen door opened behind Isabel. She stood motionless for a moment, and then, very slowly, she turned. She allowed herself one long moment to hold the sight of Wade, to let her gaze move over his mouth, his shoulders. She turned her back to him.

He came striding around to face her. "Isabel . . ." he said. For the first time, the sound of her name was soft, sweet. He reached for her hands.

She drew back from him, her body swaying back and forth. "No . . ."

The lines were deep around his eyes, but he wouldn't let go her hands as their bodies swayed in unison, to and fro, like the beginning of some dance to some music long familiar. "Isabel . . ."

Miss Ada spoke. "Leave her be, Wade. She's not here for seeing you."

Wade cupped his hand beneath Isabel's chin, making her look up at him. But it also made the tears spill from her eyes and drip onto his fingers. "I'm here to tidy up the house for Dad," she said, "that's all . . . that's all."

Now as Wade looked on the girl, sweat broke out on his forehead, almost as if her tears had flowed right through his body. "Well, you're not to go up there alone, you heah? Wait for me. Wait now 'til I cut the boiler back at the gin." He walked quickly to the door, but then he hesitated, looking back at Isabel as he held open the screen.

She brushed at her eyes. "No . . ." She turned her back to him.

"Wade," Miss Ada said. "You're lettin' in the flies!"

Isabel stood, her head bowed, as the sound of his footsteps faded from the porch. She looked at Miss Ada. "If you'd please sell me some coffee, sugar, a little flour . . ."

"You aimin' to carry it yourself? That and the suitcase, too?"

For the first time, Mother spoke. "We're going that way," she said. "We'll help carry something."

Miss Ada glanced up at those buckets, back to Isabel. "Now, Isabel," she said, "this here's the new teacher. She's a widow-lady, and she's got her own troubles. I'd advise you . . ."

Mother interrupted, "But it's no trouble, really. We'll just come for our jars tomorrow."

So, sighing, Miss Ada filled the order, and while other folks stood back watching, Mother and Polly and I left the store with Isabel and went on out to the road.

The dust rose and followed at our heels, like an old dog waiting.

The sun was low on the ridge as we passed the stand of cottonwoods and rounded the bend in the road. Here, the trees hid us from the view of the store. Isabel, looking relieved, eased her suitcase down in the dust and rubbed at her elbow. She motioned toward a fallen log there beside the road. "Let's rest a minute," she said. And while she and Mother sat on the log, with Isabel thanking Mother for helping her and Mother saying she was glad to, Polly and I stood looking at Isabel.

44

Her eyes were misty, her lips pale. She had un-
clasped the mouth of the fox and laid it across her
lap. I moved closer. "Could I pet it?"

She smiled, handed me the long, limp body.

"Did you shoot it?" I said.

"I borrowed it," she said. She turned to Mother.
"I wanted to look prosperous, as if I was no longer
the victim of bad luck." She shook her head. "But . . .
but it didn't work, did it? They still act afraid of me.
They think trouble's contagious." She sighed. "And
I-I can't blame them, after all that's happened."

"But you seem like a sensible girl," Mother said.
"Surely you don't believe that the willow tree put a
curse on the McFarlands!"

"I didn't at first." Isabel dug her nails into the
rough bark of the log. "But there was trouble . . .
you know about that, I guess. And there may be more
yet . . ." She looked up toward the ridge. The sun
was down now. The valley was filling with shadows.
"I must hurry." She stood up, lifted the sacks, jug-
gling them in her left arm as she picked up the suitcase. "I must go on alone now."

Mother frowned. "Why don't you wait 'til morning? Come stay the night with us."

Isabel shook her head. She didn't want to involve
us, she said. She couldn't allow that. But neither
could Mother allow this weary girl to carry this load
all by herself. We could at least help her to her
house. We could still get back home before dark. So,

again, we picked up the sacks, and the four of us started on up the road.

As we neared the old McFarland place, the whip-poorwills had begun their evensong, fireflies were flickering in the woods, and the wind was rising, whispering through the branches of the willow. We paused, listening. But then Mother walked straight up the rutted lane, up onto the porch.

Isabel was clutching the key in her hand, and now as she pushed at the door, it groaned slightly, as if she'd disturbed its sleep. Isabel turned to Mother. "Thank you," she said. "You must go back now."

"I will," Mother said. "But just let me light the lamp." She took the kerosene lamp down from the mantle, but the glass base was empty, the wick dry. "Do you have some candles?"

Isabel searched through the drawer of a table, found a candle and matches. She dripped tallow into a saucer, stuck the candle in it. Her hand was trembling. Her own shadow, larger than life, was a writhing ghost behind her.

"Isn't there some kerosene somewhere?" Mother said. She picked up the saucer, holding the light steady, as she and Isabel searched the kitchen, the pantry. They found nothing. "Maybe out in the barn . . ."

Isabel caught hold of Mother's arm. "Oh no. Not the barn!"

The shadows swayed, moved up closer to all of us.

"Tomorrow," Isabel said, "tomorrow I'll look in the barn. It'll be so, so dark there now."

Mother hesitated. She seemed now to be facing her own fear, as well as Isabel's. "But you'll soon be in the dark here with no lamp." She started toward the back door. "As long as we've come this far . . ."

We walked, holding hands, across the back lot, down to the barn.

It was an old, dilapidated building smelling of hay and rotted manure. Light from the moon was filtering through the high-pitched roof, and as we peered inside we saw rusted pitchforks leaning against empty stalls, an old haywagon abandoned with the hay still in it. There was hay, too, scattered across the dirt floor, and, as we moved cautiously into the barn, the hay went s-s-sh . . . s-s-sh . . . beneath our feet.

Mother was holding the candle, holding to Polly and me lest we step on a pitchfork. But now that Isabel was inside the barn, she moved faster, turning over wooden crates, picking up empty feed sacks. Then we saw she'd grabbed the end of a ladder and was dragging it toward the loft. She stepped on the first rung, started to climb.

It was then we heard the Model T rattling up the lane, the horn honking, and Wade's voice calling out "Isabel? Isabel?"

Here inside the barn, it was so still we could hear Isabel breathing. But she didn't answer.

"Is-a-bel-l-l!" Louder now.

Silence.

Then, suddenly, a wild, tormented screech tore through the barn. It was an owl high in the rafters. It was our own screams, rising in terror. It was a nightmare in which we stood petrified, unable to run, as a hoard of bats came swooping down from the loft—black, furious bodies flying toward the candlelight. Isabel leaped, screaming, from the ladder and stumbled against Mother. It was then the saucer fell from Mother's hand. The flame poured out over the hay.

The fire was like something alive, grabbing at the straw, racing across the barn floor, licking at the haywagon. The smoke was thick, acrid, burning in our lungs as we tried to scream.

But Wade had heard us. He was swinging wide the barn door and leading us out. He was grabbing empty milk buckets, handing them to Mother and Isabel, shouting for them to run to the creek for water. He ripped off his shirt, beating at the flames that were beginning to spread out from the barn. He called out to Polly and me. "Run to the car. Honk the horn. Keep it honking!"

We ran, pushing the horn over and over 'til it echoed through the hills . . . oo-gah . . . oo-gah . . . the hoarse cry of a banshee.

And finally came the answering clang of the bell

in the schoolyard. Someone had heard, had seen the smoke rising, was sounding the alarm. Soon, folks with buckets and pitchforks came running up the lane, all wide-eyed and breathless. Miss Ada came running, too, still wearing her store apron.

While Wade headed the bucket brigade, Miss Ada worked with the women, raking fast to get the dry brush back away from the barn.

At last, the smoke was subsiding, the fire coming under control. Now only the haywagon was smoldering inside the barn. Folks stood back to watch as Wade and some boys rushed into the barn, grabbed the tongue of the wagon, pulled it out into the barn lot. The men were waiting, ready with their buckets. They sloshed water onto the wagon while Wade ran back into the barn, beating out the last of the flaming straw.

Suddenly, a smoldering board collapsed from the wagon bed. A black metal box fell hissing into the mud.

Isabel turned pale. "Oh, no . . . no . . ." She ran forward, bent over, as if she would pick it up.

But the men were crowded around, drenching it, while the box steamed and hissed, like it was fighting back. Finally the men took a wrench to it, pried it open.

Miss Ada was standing up close, right there beside Isabel. She looked down into the contents of that box, and then she nodded, saying nothing, not needing to say anything. It was her cashbox, her cash, stolen by that rascal McFarland.

Isabel put her hands to her face. Her mouth stretched wide, as if she were screaming and screaming, but no sound came. She bent over, her arms tight over her ribs, as if the pain would burst her insides.

It hurt to watch her. And then, as folks looked on this fearful sight, they edged back away from Isabel, not wanting to get too close. It was Miss Ada who continued to stand beside her. It was Miss Ada who spoke. "Isabel McFarland," she said. "Hush takin' on!"

But sobs shook Isabel's body. "But-but he really *did* do it. My father *is* a thief . . . and I-I can't bear it."

Miss Ada took hold of her arm. "You got to bear it!"

Isabel said, "Miss Ada . . . Miss Ada, I believed him at first. I just *had* to!" She choked down a sob. "But then he started talking about coming back here . . . insisting on it. And I-I remembered he'd come in by the barn t-that night. So I-I decided to come search before he could." Tears streamed from her eyes as she looked at Miss Ada. "I would've given it back, every cent, honest." She shook her head, crying. "And now you won't believe me . . . now . . ."

"Now I got it back," Miss Ada said. "Hush takin' on. You're actin' just like a McFarland!"

The wind was rising, the willow branches were

whipping against the old house. You couldn't help but hear it. And as Miss Ada stood silently looking at Isabel, the girl turned and looked toward the sound.

"The McFarlands had bad luck," Isabel said. "I didn't believe that either at first. But it's true. Out here, they had cause to weep." And she was weeping now.

Miss Ada paid no mind to the willow. She was frowning at Isabel. "Under every roof there's cause to weep," she said, "sure as the wind blows. This'n ain't no different. But the McFarlands let trouble get the best of 'em and brought their suffering onto others. And I'll not have you do that to Wade, you heah? I'll not have it!"

Even now, Wade was backing out from the smoke-filled barn. He was nearly bent double with coughing. As he straightened and turned around, folks saw that his face was streaked with soot, his eyes red. But that was nothing compared to the pain on his face as he looked on the girl he loved, the girl who stood there crying. There, before him, was the evidence of McFarland's thievery. There was his ma who'd known all the time that Isabel's pa was a rascal. There were all the folks of Willow Creek, witnessing to the girl's shame.

Miss Ada was tugging off her apron, pushing it into Isabel's hands. "Now wipe your face," she said. "Wipe it quick!"

And Isabel did. She grasped that apron, scrubbed

at her face, pushed back her hair. Then she was running over the mud in the barn lot, running to Wade, touching her fingers to his mouth before he could speak. "It's all right," she said, gentle-like. "I'll be all right."

She lifted her arms to his bare shoulders, put her cheek against his. And their bodies rocked slowly together while the whippoorwills sang their evensong and the crickets chirred softly in the grass.

So this was the night when Isabel went home with the Sanders, and the next day there was a FOR SALE sign planted alongside the old McFarland place.

There on the sign was written "Inquire at Store," and that's how folks learned that Isabel said the place rightfully belonged to her pa, and he could take whatever it'd bring and get a fresh start up North. She would stay here and help Wade and Miss Ada.

Now the days were growing short, the cool breath of fall coming on the hills. So folks took to walking by the old McFarland place, looking up at the tall willow, noticing that the long gray branches were beginning to dry, the leaves drifting down on the wind.

Its season for weeping was past.

4

When the strangers came to our community, loneliness was already there, settled in for the winter. Now the wind was sighing through the hills, trees wore patches of dirty snow, and every field was cold and bare, as if even Mother Nature had abandoned us.

Few folks traveled the muddy road these days, fearing their trucks and wagons would get mired up in it. Few even walked to the store 'less they had good cause. So, as always, when the temperature went down, our lines of communication did too. And if it hadn't been for Billy Bob Pierson, it might've been spring before folks learned much about the strangers.

Billy Bob was a thin sapling of a boy a year older than I. But he was not one of the strangers. He was a Pierson, and they were as firmly rooted in these hills as dogwood and sassafras.

The Piersons were our closest neighbors. During the winter, we could look yonder past the bare trees and see the peaked roof of their house, and sometimes when the wind was right, we could even hear their flock of guineas fussing around up there.

Mrs. Pierson was the only woman in Willow Creek who kept guineas, and somehow that was typical of her. Those guinea hens were like stoop-shouldered women wearing polka-dot dresses, constantly complaining to each other about their lot in life. They were enough like Mrs. Pierson to be kinfolks.

Mr. and Mrs. Pierson were Billy Bob's grandparents, and this was apparently a constant trial to all concerned. Folks said that the Piersons were old and set in their ways, and their son ought never to have sent that rambunctious boy out here to live with them.

But Mother took the position that Mrs. Pierson really meant well, that of course she loved her grandson. She'd just forgotten the ways of children. So, during the early fall, Mother often urged Mrs. Pierson to come see us and bring Billy Bob. Then she'd get out her good china teapot, and they'd visit over cups of fragrant tea, while Billy Bob and Polly and I giggled over hot chocolate and pecan cookies.

But now winter had closed in, and their visits were less frequent. A palpable silence had come on the hills, and the small frame houses of Willow Creek were like foundlings, detached from the outside world.

Mother attempted to brighten up our house, making ruffled curtains from the flour sacks Miss Ada had given her. She got some dried pussy willows, set them in a vase near the hearth. But dusk came early, graying the curtains, and then she lit the coal-oil lamp and put records on the Victrola.

She would crank the Victrola vigorously, singing words to the music that seemed to lift her up, carry her back to happier times. But I was too young to remember the happier times, and I'd sit on the linoleum, gazing into the fire, pretending that the shifting logs were warm castles, bright with people.

Sometimes Polly and I would sit straddle-legged on the floor, playing jacks. But on Sunday afternoons I'd stand at the window, hoping the weather would allow Mrs. Pierson to appear on the road, that Billy Bob would be coming to play with us.

We never played well together, but we played loud. He would submit, at first, to a quiet game of Rook. But soon as he'd gulped down some hot chocolate, he'd pull a dried frog or a snake's rattlers from his pocket, and I'd go squealing and running around the chairs, knocking over the vase of pussy willows.

Whenever this happened, his grandma never even looked up from her crocheting. She simply shook her head and declared she didn't know what on earth was to become of that boy!

"The Lord never intended a woman my age to be raising a young'un," she'd say, rocking nearer the fire.

Apparently the Lord confided in Mrs. Pierson, for she was forever shaking her head, pursing her lips, saying, "Well now, the Lord *never* intended . . ."

I never knew what He'd intended to do about Billy Bob's parents. The only clue Mrs. Pierson ever gave to what had happened was the time she leaned toward Mother, pursed her lips, and whispered that the boy's mother "hennaed her hair," which obviously explained the whole thing.

This seemed also to explain that curious, impulsive streak in the boy which his grandma bemoaned as she told of his carryings-on. She'd tell about the time Billy Bob pulled up scarecrows from the neighbors' fields and grouped 'em around the Piersons' porch, like they was kinfolks. That episode had embarrassed his grandma 'most to tears.

"Aw, but I took 'em all back!" he'd say, turning to her when I stopped to catch my breath. "And I took the snake back to the woods, too!" he'd say, before she could repeat the story of discovering a green snake coiled up in a box beneath his bed.

Heaven only knew what else that boy had done, for she never finished recounting her trials in this world before they had to get bundled up and start home 'fore dark.

Dusk gave little warning before darkness closed in over the valley, and though lamps from distant houses were visible through the bare trees, each house was isolated by its own sea of mud and barren fields, and the weather kept folks reined close to their own hearths.

So, partly because of the weather, partly because

of the strangers themselves, it was a while before folks knew who was living on the old McFarland place.

They knew that the place had not been sold and that McFarland had refused to go back up north 'til he had found somebody to make him an offer on the place. So Wade had helped him get a job in Town at the feedstore and had encouraged him to look for some sharecroppers to work his land. Then, feeling they'd done all they could for McFarland, Wade and Isabel were married. Now in January, when there was little work to be done out here, they'd gone on their wedding trip. They were down in Biloxi, Mississippi, when Miss Ada received a curt note from McFarland saying that if she saw a light in the old house, it was sharecroppers come to live on the place.

So when folks saw smoke coming from the stone chimney, a mule scratching against the fence post, they didn't pay it much mind. Sharecroppers would more'n likely just dig a few stones from the field and then load up their mule again and go rattling off.

So no one climbed the hill to lend 'em a hand or carry 'em a sack of cracklings. And the strangers received no welcome, not even from the land itself.

It was too early for spring to make any promises, and even the groundhog had seen his shadow and burrowed back into the earth. So, to each of us who lived that winter in the hill country, loneliness appeared in many forms, wore many faces. And yet, had it not been for Billy Bob, we might never have recognized it in the boy called Joe.

I do not remember his last name. I remember only that it was difficult to pronounce, different from the names normally written on mailboxes along the road.

He first appeared at school in February, after the term had started. And he even arrived late on that first day when he came to Miss Wilkins' room. We had just finished pledging allegiance to the flag and were still standing, waiting for Miss Wilkins to signal us to be seated, when the outside door opened.

The flag fluttered in the cold draft, and we children widened our eyes to see who was to be scolded for being tardy. But Miss Wilkins kept her gaze riveted on us.

Miss Wilkins, presumably, had a heart, but she appeared to use it solely for pumping blood into her face. She had a florid complexion, hair the color of rust, and a figure that she attempted unsuccessfully to coerce with a corset.

Now she tapped the bell twice with her ruler and waited for the shuffling noises to cease. She turned and looked toward the open door.

An olive-skinned man in a red jacket and wool cap stood there. A dark-haired boy was hanging back behind him.

The man's mouth was slightly open, his breathing labored, as he waited for Miss Wilkins to speak. When she didn't, he removed his cap, twisting it in his hands, as he said, "The boy . . ." reaching back and pulling the boy forward, ". . . he has come to the school."

He tugged again at the balking boy, put his wool cap back on, and turned to go. The wind caught the door, banging it behind him, and the boy was left standing there, looking down at the floor.

Miss Wilkins said, "What's your name?"

Without lifting his head he muttered something that began "Joe . . ."

Miss Wilkins shrugged, resigned herself. "What grade are you in?"

The boy looked up at Miss Wilkins. The muscles of his throat tightened as he tried to swallow. His coat collar was turned up, but still his throat was exposed, and his arms dangled inches below the sleeves. His dark gaze turned slowly around the room. Finally he pointed to the row by the windows where the big boys were sitting. "That one," he said.

But it happened that the only vacant desk that day was next to mine. Miss Wilkins pointed her ruler. "Sit there for now," she said.

In the hush of the classroom, Joe's shoes squeaked as he walked into the girls' section and slid into the seat across from me.

Miss Wilkins turned her attention to the blackboard, and now the room was silent except for the sound of chalk scraping, until, from over near the windows, there came the sound of a snicker.

It was only a slight sound, like the quivering of leaves before a storm strikes. But that storm had been gathering for weeks now, when we weren't allowed to go outside and chase each other around the schoolyard, when recess was spent marching 'round and 'round the classroom while Miss Wilkins tapped her bell to mark cadence. But now there was a boy sitting in with the girls, and the sound of snickering swept over the classroom.

Miss Wilkins' head whipped around. "Billy Bob Pierson!" she snapped.

It's possible that Billy Bob never even started it, but whenever the boys got into a ruckus, the Pierson boy usually got the blame.

"You may go to the cloakroom," she said to Billy Bob.

He stayed in his seat. "It wasn't me done it, Miss Wilkins."

Her face flushed. "It was not *I* who *did* it, Billy Bob!"

The corner of his mouth twitched. "Wasn't me neither."

Her shoulders were pumping. "Come forward!"

He rose, walked up the aisle, put out his hand, palm turned up. Miss Wilkins grasped the ends of his fingers, bent back his palm 'til it was white, raised her ruler.

As she began whacking his palm, Billy Bob didn't flinch. Only the muscles tightened in his jaw, and the rash of freckles darkened under his eyes.

I stared down at my tablet, my eyes stinging, as the whack of ruler against flesh continued ten times. Finally it was over, and Billy Bob pushed his hands into his pockets, blinked rapidly, and then sauntered back to his seat.

I looked over at Joe. His dark cowlick had fallen over his forehead as he studied the top of his desk, tracing the carvings over and over with his finger.

Now Miss Wilkins said, "All right fourth, turn to page ten in geography."

I let out my breath and opened my arithmetic book to study. The opening of books created a background of noise. Joe leaned over to me. "Lemme look with you," he whispered.

I shook my head.

Joe had a way of narrowing his eyes so that he peered through a slat of dark lashes. "Don't then, stingy!" he said, turning away.

"But I don't *have* one," I whispered. I tried to get his attention. "I'm not in fourth grade, see?"

Suddenly I realized that Miss Wilkins was towering over me. "Were you talking?" she demanded.

I stared at her steel-encased stomach. I struggled for breath. "Yes, ma'am."

"Stand up," she said.

My knees shook. I was a thin, studious child who always wanted Mother to be proud of me, who tried to follow her advice to "be a nice girl." I didn't know what to do when my knees shook, except try to stand.

"You may go sit in the cloakroom," Miss Wilkins said, "until you can learn not to disrupt my class."

I'd seen other children banished to the cloakroom, but it never appeared to be as bad as trying not to cry while your palm was whacked. But that day, as I went alone to that small room, sat in the semi-darkness on that single wooden bench, I wished I'd known enough to sass Miss Wilkins like Billy Bob did. But then he'd been sent to that room before, he knew what it was like, and this was my first time.

There was a separate cloakroom for Miss Wilkins' room, as well as for Mother's room, and this one was hardly bigger than a closet, heavy with the smell of dampness, of coats ringed with sweat. Miss Wilkins had left the door partially open, but I couldn't see Polly's desk from here, and as I sat there in partial darkness, the other children couldn't see me well enough to make faces at me or shame me by rubbing their forefingers together.

I gazed at the coats hanging from hooks around the wall, and tried to pretend they were people in there with me. But their arms hung limp and lifeless, and finally I put my face against the cold bench and cried.

It seemed I'd been there forever before Miss Wilkins loomed in the doorway and asked if I thought I could behave now.

I wiped my face on my sleeve. "Yes'm," I said. And when I returned to my desk, the fourth grade was still on geography.

The rest of the day dragged on. Miss Wilkins provided Joe with pencil and paper, gave him some tests to write, and told him to wait after school.

When our grades were finally dismissed, I hurried across the hall that separated Miss Wilkins' room from Mother's. I stood waiting outside her door, wanting to be the first to tell her what I'd done. As I stood there, blinking hard, still trying to swallow the ache in my throat, Billy Bob came up to me.

He was wearing his mail-order coat which was obviously intended to last several winters. But this was the first season for it, and the pockets reached nearly to his knees. "Hey, Mil," he called to me, "hey, Mil, looka' here!" He pushed up his sleeves like a magician, reached into his pocket, and pulled a dead mouse out by the tail.

I gasped and squealed just as Joe came out into the hall. "Lemme see that," he said to Billy Bob.

Billy Bob dropped the mouse back into his pocket. "Lemme see you get it," he grinned.

Joe narrowed his eyes, but his arms hung slovenly at his sides. He turned away from Billy Bob and looked at me. "The ole lady put you in solitary, huh?"

I shrugged. "It was nothing," I said. I tried to toss my braids, but they were caught under my coat collar. "Nobody cares about that silly ole cloakroom."

"Aw, he calls it solitary," Billy Bob said, " 'cause his pa was in prison."

Joe's eyes blazed. "Was not!"

"Was too! My grandma said so!"

The boys started scuffling just as Mother opened her door, letting out classes. They looked up, saw her, and went running off in opposite directions.

As Mother and Polly and I started across the fields toward home, I began telling her I was ashamed for having talked in class. But Polly wailed that Miss Wilkins was just the meanest woman in the whole world.

Mother patted my head, pulled my scarf up around my throat. "Miss Wilkins does the best she can," she said to us. "I guess she's never seen much love in her life."

I told her then about the new boy, but I didn't tell what Billy Bob had said. It scared me just to think of Joe's pa being in prison, and I was afraid of saying it out loud.

But other folks began to. It wasn't long before everybody knew that Mrs. Pierson had gotten a letter from kinfolks in Town telling her that McFarland had hired a former inmate to sharecrop his land.

But Miss Ada managed to keep folks calm about it. Wade and Isabel would soon be back, she said, and they'd see to it. Anyway, the strangers were bothering no one. They kept to themselves, except for sending Joe to school every day.

Miss Wilkins put Joe in the third grade with the smaller boys, though he was as tall as Billy Bob and others in fourth. And now he shied away from everybody. During lunch period, he'd take his cold sweet potato out of his desk and chew while keeping his head bent over a book, though he rarely turned a page. On warmer days, when we were sent outside for recess, Joe'd just lean back against the school building and watch the boys playing ball.

Once Billy Bob caught a ball and tossed it over toward Joe. But Joe didn't attempt to catch it, and it smashed into his face. He put his fist into his mouth, biting down on his knuckles, squeezing his eyes shut.

Billy Bob ran over to him. "Hey . . . hey, Joe, look," he said, and held out the snake's rattlers in his hand. But Joe backed away, turned and ran up the steps into the schoolhouse just as the bell was ringing to end recess.

Joe never did anything bad enough to get a licking. The only wrong thing he did was to mumble "I dunno" whenever Miss Wilkins called on him to recite. The punishment for this was to stay after school and study. But even Miss Wilkins wearied of this, and finally she quit calling on him, allowing him to grab his coat and go hightailing it down the road the minute school let out.

So within two weeks the novelty of the new boy had worn off and nothing much was said to him or about him—until the day he clashed with Miss Wilkins.

It rained intermittently that morning, as if winter and spring had begun fighting it out in the hills.

But by recess time the sky had darkened, and small hailstones peppered the ground. So we ate at our desks and then the marching began, two rows at a time.

Then it was time for the boys by the window to march, and as they paced up and down the aisles, Billy Bob was bringing up the rear. As he passed Joe's desk, Joe stuck out his foot, tripped him. Billy Bob stumbled into the boy in front of him, sent him sprawling. But this time Miss Wilkins was facing the class, tapping out cadence, and there was no mistaking who'd started the ruckus.

She marched right back to Joe. He stuck out his left hand, palm turned up. But Miss Wilkins was holding her bell, not her ruler, and she pointed her finger close to his nose. "You take your books and you march yourself right into the cloakroom!"

He slid out of his seat, pushed his hands into his pockets and started up the aisle.

"I said *take your books!*"

He kept going.

"This instant!"

Now, just outside the cloakroom, he hesitated. He screwed up his face, and then he let loose a mouthful of spit. He was turned sideways to the class, and we could see it arch up with perfect aim, drop smack on the doorsill of the cloakroom.

For an instant, Miss Wilkins was struck dumb. Then, as Joe retreated into the semi-darkness, she stalked up to the cloakroom and slammed the door!

That settled, she turned back to the class and started whamming the bell, admonishing the boys to pick up their feet and keep time.

Finally the marching was over, and one full period had passed before she missed Billy Bob.

"Where is that boy?" she said to the class.

But no one seemed to know. He had not asked to be excused, had not gone outside. He was too big to hide behind the stove, and so there was only one place left.

She walked to the door of the cloakroom. "Billy Bob Pierson, are you in there?" She flung open the door.

We could see the shadow of his head as he sat there on the bench by Joe. "Yes'm," he answered. The room was breathlessly silent as Billy Bob stood up and came to the doorway.

Standing just inside the dim cloakroom, Billy Bob looked out at Miss Wilkins. "He was in solitary, Miss Wilkins," he said. "So . . . so I sat with him. That's all I done, honest."

So that's all he'd done. But it made Miss Wilkins' face turn pale. She looked down at the floor, and suddenly I wondered if Miss Wilkins ever cried.

Now Joe stood beside Billy Bob and took a step forward. He stooped down, rubbed his sleeve over the doorsill where his spit had dried.

Softly, Miss Wilkins let out her breath. She moved over to her desk, lowered herself into her chair. "You boys take your seats," she said.

For a moment, Miss Wilkins sat at her desk, rubbing her hands across her forehead. Then she lifted her head. "Maybe we could have a little change in curriculum today," she said. She opened her desk drawer, drew out a book. "If everyone will be very quiet, I'll read you one of the classics from *Aesop's Fables*."

Everyone was quiet. But it was a gentle kind of quiet, like breathing in unison.

The next day Miss Wilkins brought in a crockery bowl with daffodil bulbs set into pebbles and promised that we'd soon see the bulbs sprout and bud. And finally spring came bustling into the hills, airing out the dogwood blossoms, fluffing up the green pastures.

It happened that the strangers didn't stay much longer in our community, for the McFarland place was sold that spring, and the sharecroppers moved on.

But the memory of that day stayed with me forever, and there are times, even now, when I can hear Billy Bob saying, "So I sat with him. That's all I done."

And then I wonder if Billy Bob, too, remembers the time we were children living in the hills. I wonder if, through the years, he retained his sensitivity, his awareness of another's feeling of aloneness. I wonder whatever became of that boy. Where is he now? What is he doing?

5

Folks in Willow Creek were forever nagging at the weather, saying it ought to stop whatever it was doing or do whatever it wasn't. Sometimes it seemed to heed them too, and there'd be a gentle rain following the planting season or a long dry spell until the last fluff of cotton was stripped from the fields.

But though folks were always passing judgment on the weather, it was hard to tell if it ever passed judgment on us. Every rain brought profit to some, pain to others, so who could say when it was falling on the just, or the unjust, or just falling.

There was that spring when the clouds burst on the ridge, and the creek became swollen and jaundiced from eating into the yellow clay hills. The rising water sucked down some of the fencing. The rain leaked through the shingled rooftops. And yet, that same storm brought the wind rushing through the cottonwood trees, tearing loose a broken limb, tossing it across the county road. And that's how it happened that the long green car with the rumble seat was stranded in our community.

Normally, the man and the woman in that long green car would've driven right on through Willow Creek, anxious to get back to the highway where they'd taken the wrong turn. They would've heard only the whistle of the train as it neared the crossing, slowing to see whether it'd be flagged down. And they'd have seen no one but Emily Long, there at the store, when they went inside to ask directions.

Emily had recently been hired to help out at the Sanderses' store. Wade and Isabel were busy building a house now, and Wade had insisted that Miss Ada get someone to spell her from those long hours at the store.

Emily was a shy, needy girl, eager to prove her worth to Miss Ada. So she would surely have tried to sell those strangers some apple cider. It was not *hard* cider and there wasn't much call for it. But more'n likely, that man would've asked for two cokes, tossed a quarter on the counter, and then gone back out to the steps where the girl stood smiling up at him as their hands touched. The long green car would've gone heading off toward the ridge, while Emily Long, still holding the man's change, stood behind the counter saying, "Well ... well I never!"

And that would've been the end of it.

If it hadn't been for the storm, that couple would scarcely have glanced at these hills, never have noticed our small frame house, much less come knocking at the door.

Our house had shed a few shingles during the

winter, and our wicker chairs had been moved inside, leaving the porch bare. It was hardly the kind of place that'd attract folks who drove a car with a rumble seat.

So if the storm hadn't brought them, I might never have seen love and romance up close like that. At least, not for a long time.

The closest I'd ever been to that kind of romance was when we lived in Town and went to the picture show where Polly and I sat on the first row, staring up at the giant-sized faces that whispered and kissed and cried while a violin played.

We'd asked Mother later why the violin made them cry, but she just shook her head, pushed her handkerchief back into her purse. "It was just part of the story," she said. "It was just make-believe."

But it was not make-believe when the man and the woman came to our house. It happened right in front of our eyes, and we were close enough to touch the shadow of beard on the man's face, to sniff the fragrance of the woman's coat. There even came a time when it seemed I heard the violin.

It began late on a Friday afternoon.

The clouds had been wrestling over us all day, but now their force was spent, and the leak from the kitchen ceiling was only an occasional drip hitting the porcelain pan.

Normally, Mother didn't light the lamp this early, but the sunset had cast an eerie glow over the clouds, so she turned up the wick and struck a match to the kerosene lamp. She threw a log on the fire, bringing out a bright gold reflection from the picture of my father there on the mantle.

Sometimes I'd stand up close to that picture, squinting my eyes 'til it seemed that his mouth moved and he smiled at me. But I had only a vague memory of him, and here in the hills I looked on men as something that hung around the store in overalls or rode through the pages of storybooks.

Then it was that Friday afternoon, just turning dusk, and suddenly there was a knock at the door.

Mother turned from the fireplace. "Now who on earth . . ."

I ran to the door, pulled it open, and there stood the tall, dark-haired man—an outsider. I lowered my head, lifted my eyes, letting my gaze creep up on him.

His shoes were caked with mud, but still you could see they were black leather, laced at the instep, unaccustomed to dirt roads. He wore a belted topcoat with the collar turned up in back but open in front so his necktie showed blue, like his eyes. There were lines around his mouth as if he were accustomed to laughing. But now there was worry wrinkling his forehead. He was looking past me to where Mother stood with Polly peeking around from behind her.

"Sorry to trouble you," he said, "but I seem to be in a real predicament."

Mother and Polly moved toward the door and leaned out, looking down the path that dog-legged in from the road.

There was the long green car with the rumble seat. And there, in front of the car, was the fallen limb of the cottonwood tree. The bare branches were spread out like fingers, like a giant's hand, blocking the road. The car door was open. A blonde woman was sitting sideways on the seat, her feet on the running board, her hair blowing in the wind.

"I can't get around it," the man was saying, "and I'm afraid of backing into the ditch. I wonder if Mr. Wasson might give me a hand?"

Mother hesitated, taking time to appraise the stranger. Finally she said, "I have no husband. There're just the girls and me."

The man rubbed his hand across his forehead. He looked out from our porch, turning his head each way, as if looking would make another house appear across the field yonder. But there was only the schoolhouse, the flag hanging wet and limp on the pole. When Mother and Miss Wilkins had seen the storm approaching, they'd let out early so children could race the cloud home. And now there was no one in sight. There only the wind coming through the woods, cold and damp, ruffling up his dark hair.

"D'you know where I might get help?"

"Well, you might try up at the Piersons'," Mother said, "but it's quite a walk in all this mud, and with dark coming on . . ."

Suddenly Mother stepped back and opened the door wide. "But do come in," she said, motioning toward the fire. "You needn't stand there in the cold."

The man bowed slightly, like a prince. "Oh no, thank you. I'd track dirt into your house."

Mother glanced down at the floor. "Why, I'd consider it a pleasure," she smiled, as if our linoleum had suddenly become a flowered carpet with a border. "Go ask your wife to come in. I'll put coffee on."

The man looked back to where the woman was sitting in the car. "Oh, she's . . . ," he began and then looked again toward Mother. "Yes, she can stay with you while I go for help."

So he turned and started back down the path. Mother hurried to the kitchen while Polly and I stayed there in the doorway, hardly feeling the cold as we watched the man leap the mud puddles and cross to the road.

He stood for a moment, talking with the woman, gesturing toward our house. She appeared to be protesting, but finally she stood out on the running board, and he lifted her into his arms and started back toward the path. He slipped, almost dropping her, and she laughed up at him, putting her forehead against his chin, her legs swinging gracefully in the crook of his arm. The wind lifted her blonde hair against his mouth as he ran laughing and sliding up to our wooden step and set her down on the porch.

She was small and fragile-looking. Her hair hung in a straight bob with a fluff of bangs across her forehead. Her skin had the delicate tint of china, and she looked, to me, like a store-bought doll, like the only good doll I'd ever owned.

That doll had been my proudest possession in Town, and when we'd come out here to the hills she'd come, too. But one day I carried her to the sand ditch to play with Polly and me. A sudden rain had come up, and we'd gone running home, forgetting the doll. By the time I could go back for her, her hair was ruined, the color was drained from her face, and her voice box was rusted out.

But the girl who stood on our porch now was beautiful and smiling as she spoke to Mother. "This is so thoughtful of you," she said.

She was wearing a black cloth coat. It didn't look as fine as I would've thought, coming out of a car with a rumble seat, but her high-heel shoes were black patent leather, and there was a strap across the instep.

Mother motioned her inside. "Why, it's so nice to have you!" she said, as if she were hostess at a party. I noticed that Mother had removed her apron and pinned a broach at her neck. "Do come in. Come in!"

The girl came walking in toward the fire while the man stooped down, unlaced his shoes, and set them outside on the porch before he walked across the linoleum.

Polly put her hand over her mouth, trying not to giggle at the sight of a man in his stocking feet.

He stood now before the hearth, and I moved closer, taking a good look. The socks were navy blue with a red stripe running up the side, and he was wiggling his toes against the warm bricks.

The blonde woman was touching my braids, and I turned and looked up at her. She tossed me a smile that was easy to return, like somebody playing catch with a beginner. "Hello there, little girl," she said. "I'm Christine, and this . . . ," turning toward the man.

"Steve Jones," he said, interrupting her. "Steve Jones from Nashville."

Her face had been radiant as she smiled at him, but when he spoke her eyes clouded.

Mother said, "Let me take your things, Mrs. Jones."

The girl shook her head. "Oh, just call me Christine."

Mother smiled. "Let me take your things, Christine."

The girl was still wearing her coat and gloves. As she stood by the fire, her movements were all in slow motion. She took off her coat, pulling first at one sleeve, then the other. She began peeling off her gloves, exposing her wrists, her hands, finally her fingers. A flush started at her throat, moving up into her cheeks as she lifted her head. Her hair swung back from her face as she turned to look at Mother.

Mother took the black coat off Christine's arm and handed it to me. "Hang our guest's coat, Mildred," she said.

There was a wonderful fragrance to that coat, sweet as lilacs, and even after I carried it into the bedroom and placed it on a hanger, I stood inside the closet and leaned against the cloth, breathing in its fragrance.

When I went back, Steve Jones was saying, "Mind if I use your phone? Maybe I can rouse the highway department."

Mother laughed. "All I can offer is coffee. The nearest phone is back down the road at the store, but I doubt anyone's there now."

He frowned. "Seems I remember it being open when we passed."

"Well, maybe you're right," Mother said. "Emily Long should've closed up early and gone home ahead of the storm, but knowing Emily . . ."

Knowing Emily, Mother knew she might well have stayed on 'til closing time before starting to sweep up. There wasn't a more conscientious worker in these parts than the shy, wren-like girl.

She had brown hair and brown eyes, and even the words she spoke were as repetitious as a bird's twittering. No matter what Emily saw or what she heard, she'd just shake her head and say, "Well . . . well, I never!"

And you knew she spoke true. Emily Long had

never done much of anything except work and look out for Bubba.

Bubba was Emily's brother. He was thirty years old—much older than Emily—and yet it was she who looked after him. Bubba was, as folks out here said, just plain no 'count. Folks said it was a disgrace the way he'd let the Long place run down after the old folks passed on. The only thing he ever really put his mind to was rolling a cigarette so the tobacco wouldn't fall out, and he didn't even do that unless Emily worked to buy his tobacco. Folks said it plain wasn't right, and sometimes when we were at the store, Mother would try what she called "talking some sense" into Emily.

"You're too young and too sweet a girl," Mother would say, "to spend your life this way." Mother would say that Emily ought to smile at Chet Daniels sometime.

Chet Daniels had just bought the old McFarland place, and he was looked on as the most eligible bachelor in these parts. He was a tall, rawboned man not much given to small talk. But he worked sunup to sundown fixing up that place, and he had a few cows, a flatbed truck, and he seemed to know how to bring out the good in that land. Whenever he came into the store, all the girls would look kind of side-long at him. But Emily Long would just busy herself over the charge books, keeping her head down.

"You don't know what you're missing, Emily," Mother would say.

Always, when Chet's name was mentioned, Emily's face would get kind of pink, but she'd shake her head at Mother. "I know I promised Ma I'd always look out for Bubba," she'd say. "I can't help my feelings about that."

Apparently, she couldn't help feeling responsible for the store either, and so, although the storm would keep folks off the road, Emily would be sure to stay on 'til closing time.

"She'll probably be there a little while yet," Mother said now to Steve Jones. Then she got the lantern from the kitchen and handed it to him. "It'll be dark before you're back."

Christine went with him out on the porch, and I stood in the doorway watching them, hoping to see him kiss her good-bye, wondering if violins would play. But he only said, "I won't be long," and she put her forehead against his chin, saying, "Take care."

Mother was pulling at the back of my dress, saying, "Child, child." But I was seeing romance close up, and I stood there until he went down the porch and Christine came back in, closing the door behind us.

She walked over to the fireplace and leaned her arms on the mantle, watching the fire.

Mother said, "Won't you take supper with us? I've made soup."

Christine turned. Her hair was the color of firelight, but there were shadows under her eyes. "I'm not hungry," she said.

"Well, I'll just feed the girls," Mother said. "And when your . . . ," she spoke softly, her words gentle as a touch, "when your Mr. Jones gets back, we'll fry up some ham, all right?"

Mother got two bowls, filled them with soup, set them on the round table. The table was in the center room now, for the kitchen was drafty in winter and the spring rains had caused the ceiling to leak. But this room was warm, and with the table, the wicker chairs, the Victrola set on the fern stand, it looked cheerful and well furnished, as if it were planned that way.

As Polly and I ate, Mother pulled two chairs up nearer the hearth, and she and Christine sat there sipping coffee. They spoke briefly of the weather and the roads, but mostly they just gazed into the fire as if they were searching for something to talk about.

In the silence, we heard the wind rising, the woods moaning. The trees were scratching against the roof, like something trying to sneak in. Suddenly, an owl hooted at the night.

Christine shivered. "Oh my! Aren't you afraid out here all alone?"

Mother held her hands out toward the fire. "I try not to be," she said. "But sometimes . . ." She moved her chair closer to Christine, as if she had a sudden compulsion to share her thoughts with this girl from

80

the outside. "Sometimes I just can't help being afraid, but ..."

Christine nodded. She looked up at the picture of my father, there on the mantle. "But I guess you had no choice."

Mother put her hand on Christine's arm. "Oh, but I did," she protested. "I had a choice." She glanced back at Polly and me. "I chose to make a home for my girls." She stood up quickly, poked at the fire, breaking the wood 'til it flamed up. "I'll get some hot coffee," she said.

When she came back carrying the coffeepot, she was also carrying small, white napkins, crocheted on the edges. I'd never seen those dainty napkins before, nor had I ever noticed the graceful way Mother poured the coffee and then seated herself, smoothing her skirt, holding her cup with her fingers curved.

She smiled at Christine. "Have you ever come this way before?" she said, her voice bright.

But Christine didn't smile. "No. No, never!" She pushed the hair back from her cheek and leaned forward, looking into Mother's face. "Honest, I never have before!"

"Oh, dear, I wasn't prying. I didn't mean ..."

"I know you didn't," Christine said, "but I wanted you to know." She sighed, "I don't suppose you could understand." They both turned back to the fire as the wood shifted and flamed. Mother said, "I think I can. He's a very attractive man."

"Oh, yes! Isn't he?" Christine smiled. "Why, every

girl in the office . . . every woman who ever *sees* him . . . you know?"

"Yes, he's very attractive."

"Oh, and I love him, you see?" Christine's voice trembled. "I just can't help loving him."

They sat silent for a moment. I kept listening for them to start talking again, and when they didn't, I spoke up. "He's like a prince, isn't he?"

Mother turned suddenly, as if my voice startled her, as if she were surprised to see Polly and me sitting there at the table.

She and Christine exchanged a look, and then Mother said, "Why don't we pop some corn? Wouldn't that be fun?"

So she got out the wire popper, and we took turns shaking it over the grate. Then Mother boiled up some molasses, and we buttered our fingers and made popcorn balls, setting them on the buttered platter. They were just beginning to harden when we heard footsteps on the porch.

Christine ran to the door, threw it open. She smiled, seeing the tall man standing there.

And there, standing beside him, was Emily Long.

Emily came in quickly, her bright eyes darting around the room as if she were looking for a place to light. She was bundled into her brown coat, a wool scarf around her throat, and she was carrying the lantern, for now Steve was carrying two big paper sacks.

He handed the sacks to Christine while he stooped

down to remove his muddy shoes. Emily dashed over to Mother and grasped her hands. "Bubba'll be along," she said breathlessly. "He'll be along soon!"

Mother looked puzzled. "What, Emily?"

Steve was inside now. "Emily says her brother will be able to lend us a hand."

"That's so!" Emily said in a voice loud and strained, not at all like Emily. "I've been expecting Bubba to bring the wagon down to ride me home. So . . . so I just closed the store and left a note for him on the door, told him to come quick as he could." She nodded her head vigorously, gasped as if she'd been running. "He'll be along soon!"

Steve was setting the sacks on the round table. "And now, while we're waiting . . ." He began unloading the sacks. Licorice whips. Horehound drops. Bottles of creme soda.

Mother said, "Let me take your coat, Emily." So Emily unwound her scarf and looped it through the sleeve of her coat.

Our house was filled with excitement, like a party, and proudly I walked over and took Emily's coat, just as I'd taken Christine's.

But Emily's coat smelled of feed sacks and coal oil, so different from Christine's with the fragrance of lilacs. As I carried it into the bedroom, I stepped inside the dark closet, wanting once again to put my face against Christine's coat, to breathe in the sweetness. So it happened that I was hidden there when I heard Emily's voice whispering to Mother in the bedroom. I had to strain my ears to catch what she was saying.

"But when he telephoned to someone named Martha and said he was delayed in Town on *business* . . ."

I heard Mother say, "Oh?"

"And he wouldn't be back until Monday!" Emily gasped. "Well, I was afraid for you here alone! Course I didn't know about that woman with him!"

Mother said, "Sh-h-h."

But once Emily had started, she couldn't be stopped. "He even asked Martha about the *children* . . . didn't know I heard 'im . . . or didn't care."

Mother said, "Oh!" as if it hurt.

Emily said, "What are you going to *do?*"

Mother didn't get a chance to answer, for now Christine called out, "Shouldn't Steve bring in some firewood?"

Emily said to Mother, "Well, let's just hope Bubba comes!" And they left the bedroom.

I stood there in the dark, holding to the sleeve of Christine's coat. And suddenly I was afraid. Something was going to happen. They were going to do something to Christine, and I didn't know what or why.

But while I stood there, I heard Mother saying she was going to fry up some ham, and I heard Steve Jones talking and laughing, and so I went back, and they'd not missed me. Now Steve was tossing a popcorn ball to Polly, and she was giggling.

When the ham and biscuits were ready, Mother,

Emily, Christine, and Steve sat down to the table while Polly and I sat on the floor playing jackstraws. Emily was quiet, as usual, but the others talked easily, laughing occasionally. So the knot in my stomach began to melt, and it seemed now that nothing bad was going to happen.

When the dishes were cleared, Mother said, "We *do* have a Victrola," as if that were much better than having a telephone. She put a record on, I ran to crank it, and the man's voice sang, "I met my love in Avalon . . . beside the sea."

Steve smiled, held out his arms to Christine, and she went to him, putting her face close to his, singing softly with the music. As they began to dance, it seemed that their feet hardly touched the floor, and there was only a slight swishing sound as they moved over the linoleum.

Mother and Emily sat in the chairs near the fire, watching the dancers. Mother's shoulders were swaying in time, but Emily sat straight, her hands clasped in her lap. She said, "Wouldn't you think Bubba could've come looking for me by now?"

Mother said, "Yes."

"Course, you know bad weather is kinda' hard on Bubba. He doesn't much take to getting out when it's bad."

Mother said, "I know."

The song was finished now, the record going around soundlessly. Mother got up to change it, letting Polly crank it this time. Now the voice sang

out "When the red, red robin comes bob, bob, bobbin'
along . . . a-long . . ."

Mother looked toward Steve. "Do dance with
Emily," she smiled.

Emily's mouth fell open. "Oh my, no!"

Steve held out his arms to her.

She blushed to the roots of her hair. "Oh, no!"

Steve threw back his head and laughed. He leaned
over, put his hands around Emily's waist, swept her
right up off her chair.

"Oh my!" Emily said. The pins were coming loose
from her dark hair. Wisps sprang out over her ears.

Steve placed her left arm on his shoulder, took
her right hand in his. "Why, I . . ." Emily gasped.
"Why, I never!"

Steve whirled her around in his arms. Once in a
while her toes would bounce against the linoleum,
but it was hard to tell whether she was trying to get
her feet back down on the floor or whether she was
trying to dance. Finally, Steve whirled Emily back to
her chair and eased her down into it. He bowed to
her. "It was a pleasure," he smiled.

Emily was gasping for breath, pushing her hair
back from her ears. Her right cheek looked pink
where it had been scratched by his chin. She put
her palm against her cheek, touching the warmth
of it.

I said to Mother, "Do *we* get to dance, too?"

She shook her head. "It's very late. Little girls
should get to bed." When Polly and I started to wail

with protest, she said, "I thought you might like for Christine to tuck you in."

So Christine took hold of Polly's hand and of mine and led us into the cool bedroom. I showed her where our flannel nightgowns were hung and where the hairbrush was. And then I sat on the edge of the bed, my legs folded up under me, watching Christine as she unwound Polly's braids and began to brush.

I searched my mind for something to say, wanting to make grown-up conversation. "How old are *your* children?"

She was brushing so gently that Polly wasn't even complaining. She smiled at me. "I don't have any children."

"Why not?" I said. "If Steve has children, why don't you?"

She opened her mouth, making a hollow, gasping sound, as if her voice box wouldn't work.

Something strange was happening to her, and somehow it was my fault, and I didn't know what to do. "I mean . . ." I said, "Emily Long said that he . . ." I stopped, sensing that this was wrong, too.

Christine sat motionless, looking at me. "That he . . ." she repeated, waiting.

"That he called about the children," I said.

The color drained from her face. Her arms hung limp, her eyes were glassy. She was a china doll, left in the rain.

My throat was hurting. There was a pounding in my ears. Then I realized that the pounding was coming from the porch, from the front door. "Don't go," I said to Christine. "Don't go away."

She put the hairbrush down on the dresser, patted Polly's head. Then she leaned over to me, put her cool cheek against mine. She walked into the other room, and I followed her.

Chet Daniels was standing at the door, crushing the brim of his hat in his hands. "Is help needed?" he said to Mother. And to Emily, "I read your note."

Emily was blushing. "I- I meant it for Bubba."

Chet nodded. "My cows got through the fence," he said. "I've been out getting 'em off the tracks 'fore the train comes through. When I passed the store, I saw there was a note on the door and figured I ought to read it."

"I-I figured Bubba'd come for me," Emily said, as if she'd forgotten all about the car on the road.

Chet looked at Steve Jones. "I guess you're the one needs help," he said. "I've got rope in the truck."

Steve got his coat, took the lantern, and the two men went down the path, over to the road. We stood at the window, watching. The moon was high now, lighting the hills, and the valley was a pewter bowl.

Now it was only a matter of time until the men had the rope under that fallen limb. The road would be cleared. Christine would be gone away forever. I reached for her hand. "Please don't go," I said. "I don't want you to go!"

Mother said, "Child, child."

But my throat was hurting. I could taste salt on my mouth. "I don't want her to go!" I was bawling like a calf.

Mother shook my shoulder. "Hush now! You mustn't feel like that."

But I wouldn't hush. "I can't help how I feel . . . nobody can . . . not even you or Emily or Christine. That's what you all say . . . and I can't either!"

Mother kept her hand on my shoulder, patting me. "I guess we did say that, didn't we?"

I turned around, looking up at her. But she wasn't looking at me. She was looking at Christine, at Emily. "And I guess it's true," she said. "I guess none of us can help how we feel." She hesitated, listening to the wind sigh outside the house. The branches were scratching against the roof, the owl hooting at the night. "But I guess we can help what we do about it," she said.

The room was quiet. We could hear the shifting of the fire, the men's shouts echoing back to us.

We watched from the window until the road was cleared and the men returned to the house.

Steve came in first. "All clear," he said. "We can head on to Nashville now."

Chet stood at the door, his hat in his hands, saying, "Be glad to ride you home, Emily."

Mother had brought in the coats. She handed them to Christine and Emily. But as Christine began pulling on her gloves, she turned away from Steve Jones and looked at Chet. "You say the train is due along soon?"

Chet nodded. "But it's not going to Nashville. Going back the other way."

Christine fastened her coat. "And it'll stop here? For me?"

"If we flag it down," Chet said. "If we hurry."

Steve was frowning at Christine. "Say now, what's this? What d'you mean? I-I thought . . ."

"I know," Christine said softly. "I thought so, too, for a while."

The color rose in his face. "Quit your kiddin'." He grasped her wrist, pulling her toward the door.

She shook her head, pried his fingers from her wrist one at a time, as if it took all her strength to do it. "I'm going back, Steve."

Finally he shrugged, turned, and walked out, leaving the door ajar. Christine leaned against the door, watching him as he went on down the path, crossed to the road, and got into the car.

Chet Daniels had taken Emily's coat. He held it out to her, waiting.

Emily was looking out toward the road. "Well . . ." she said. "Well, I never!"

But as the long green car started its motor and roared away, Emily put her hand to her cheek. Very slowly, she turned and looked kind of sidelong at Chet Daniels. And that was the moment when Emily Long looked as if, someday, she just might.

6

If the fearful news had come from anyone other than a Pierson, the men in the store would've interrupted their checker game, rushed home for their shotguns, and spread out to search the hills.

But when Billy Bob Pierson came running into the store on a gray winter afternoon, shouting, "A man escaped from the road gang! Grandma sent me to warn everybody," nobody paid him much mind.

It wasn't that they doubted Mrs. Pierson had sent him, or that she was, as he said, home right now barring the doors.

Mrs. Pierson was, in her own words, a "God-fearing woman," and if she said there was danger a-comin', she believed it to be the gospel truth. But folks in Willow Creek looked on Mrs. Pierson as a tense woman, with the nervous habit of glancing back over her shoulder as if she feared the Holy Ghost was about to pounce on 'er. And if *she* had written the Gospel, it would've read: "Watch! For you know neither the day, nor the hour, nor what cometh next!"

Now Billy Bob rushed over to Miss Ada. "She says he's sure to be headin' this way!"

Miss Ada just sighed. "Saints preserve us," she said, but in a perfunctory sort of way, as if she were asking to be preserved from Mrs. Pierson rather than from any real danger.

"Yes'm," Billy Bob agreed breathlessly. "Grandpa just came in from Town. He says there's all sorts of commotion back yonder at the levee. That's where the road gang was workin' when the man sprung loose."

One of the men glanced up from the checker game. "Well, boy, that fella's probably clean to Arkansas by now."

Billy Bob turned back to the counter. "Grandma says you'd best have your shotgun ready, Miss Ada. The fella's probably a killer!"

"Now, Billy Bob," Miss Ada said, "they don't likely have killers out on the road gang. Anyway, we're a right smart piece from the levee. He'd be caught 'fore he got this far. You go tell your grandma that now, y'heah?"

"Yes'm," he said. "I'll tell 'er." But he kept standing there, eyeing the candy counter as if he hoped Miss Ada'd reward him for running all the way down here.

But Miss Ada wasn't likely to give out candy for that. She gave candy to children only when their folks came in to settle up their bills.

Normally, this would've been the day when Polly

and I received a piece of horehound, for this was the end of the month and Mother had come in after school to cash her check. But today, as Miss Ada counted out the money, Mother had said, "I wonder if you could let my bill run on a little longer, Miss Ada. I've ordered some shoes for the children, and ..."

Miss Ada pushed the money across the counter. "Now don't you worry your head about that," she said. "Your credit's good with me." Then she smiled at Polly and me. "But it *is* the first of the month," she said, "and the girls got to have their horehound. Now if they'll just sing me one of those pretty songs ..."

I could almost taste the tart, amber candy. But I shook my head. "I don't know any."

"Why, of course you do," Mother said. "You know lots of songs!"

And that was true. During the long winter evenings when the joints of our old house started creaking, when a lonely dog howled in the distance, baying at the moon, Mother would pop corn, and the three of us would sing rounds. She'd also taught me the words to "Brighten the Corner Where You Are," and I'd sung it at a school program.

Miss Ada had been at that program, leading the applause, and now, this afternoon, she said, "C'mon now, child, sing me that pretty song!"

But I looked down at the floor and shook my head.

When Billy Bob had come in with the fearful

news, I'd thought she'd forget all about my singing. But she had dismissed him, though he was still standing there. And now she started in coaxing me again. "If you sing," she said, "I'll give you something nice."

I bit my lip. "I don't want any . . . any char-charity!"

Charity was a word I'd learned only today, but the painful sound of it still throbbed in my ears.

Today all the grades had recessed together. It had been a cold, damp day, and when the sun finally showed itself at noontime, Mother and Miss Wilkins sent all the classes outside.

I sat down on the wooden steps, opened my lunch pail, and ate my sausage and cold biscuit. I'd just taken out my fried apple pie, with the buttered crust, and sugar sprinkled over it, when a square-toothed, sixth-grade girl sashayed up to me. "Gimme," she said.

"No," I said. "It's mine!"

She grabbed the pie from my hand and bit into it. The applesauce leaked out.

I jumped up. "Give that back!"

But she was a head taller than I, and I stood helplessly watching her jaws work as she swallowed the last of it, licked her fingers.

"Was mine anyway," she said. "The apples came from *my* farm!"

"Did not!"

"Did too!' She grinned. The crust showed between her square teeth. "Everything you eat's given to ya. Everybody knows *that!*" She said it loud, making the other children turn to listen. "Your ma takes charity!"

I stamped my feet. "Does not!"

"Does. Does! Charity. Charity!"

I reached down, picked up my lunch pail, threw it at her. But it was weightless, and it only grazed her shoe. She shrieked, hopping up and down on one foot.

Mother had seen the commotion, and now she came across the schoolyard. I thought she was coming to scold the girl, but she took hold of my arm. "You know better than to throw things!"

"But she took my pie," I cried, not wanting to say the rest of it, "and she's bigger'n I am!"

"It doesn't make you any bigger to throw things," she said in the same level voice she used with other students. "You only encourage her to hurt you when you act that way."

But the girl's words *had* hurt. It was true that folks were always giving us things. I'd never really thought of it before. And this afternoon, as I stood there in the store in front of everybody with Miss Ada saying, "I'll give you something," I felt my ears burn, my face flush.

"I-I don't want any . . . any charity!" I repeated.

Polly said, "*I* do, Miss Ada," thinking it was something like horehound.

Mother picked out two nickels from the change Miss Ada had pushed over to her. She handed one to each of us. "Select what you like," she said. "Treat yourselves today."

Usually we were lucky to have a penny, and a whole nickel made my palm sweat. I sensed I'd hurt Mother, knew I should spend only a penny and save the rest, but everyone was watching. I pointed to a bar of Hershey chocolate, and Miss Ada accepted my nickel. Then, wanting to redeem myself with Mother, I peeled off the tinfoil, broke off four squares, and offered them to Billy Bob.

"Golly gee!" he said, grasping the squares. "Gee, Mil, thanks!" He closed his eyes as he gulped the warm, sweet chocolate. He wiped his mouth with the back of his hand. "I gotta' hurry," he said. "Grandma'll scalp me if'n that killer comes bustin' in 'fore I get the shotgun loaded." He went running out the store.

Miss Ada shook her head. "Poor child. That woman'll scare the daylights out of 'im. She can sure get worked up over nothing."

As we began walking home, I said, "Mother, do you think Mrs. Pierson's really scared of nothing?"

Mother laughed. "I think she's scared of everything, poor soul. But she'd probably scare an intruder worse than he'd scare her."

I stopped in my tracks. "You mean, you think he's *coming?*"

"Oh no, no, I didn't mean that. I just meant there's so much fear in her that she projects it to others sometimes. At least, she tries to. And we mustn't ever be like that."

Twilight was darkening the road. As we neared a field of dried cornstalks, a hawk swooshed down from the sky, a field mouse squealed in agony. An owl called out "Who-o-o? Who-o-o?" as if it were questioning the shadows beneath the cottonwoods. We began walking faster.

The house was damp and somber from being closed up all day. We kept our coats buttoned up while Mother poked dead ashes from the grate and laid the fire. She made a small fire, for the woodbox was running low tonight, and only one large log remained. As the room warmed, she took her month's pay from her purse, secured the bills with a rubber band, and laid them beneath the single log in the woodbox.

Mother had hidden her money in that box ever since we moved out here. Most folks in the country hid their money in the mattress or the sugar bowl, but Mother said that was no better than leaving it in plain view. She reasoned that if anyone ever did break in here while we were at school, they'd never think of searching beneath the logs in the woodbox.

So, to her, the money was safe there, just as our door was safe after she'd pushed a straight chair up under the doorknob.

That door did have a lock on it, but our old house

was always shifting, settling its joints, like it was trying to get comfortable, and the key would no longer turn in the lock. But Mother was expecting Uncle Marvin to come through in a few weeks, and he'd fix it. Until then she'd just make do by tilting the chair under the knob in case a strong wind tried to push open the door during the night.

We ate our supper huddled before the fire, but the wind kept sucking the heat up the chimney, and though our faces were hot, our backs were cold. Finally, when the fire burned low, Mother banked the grate with ashes. "We may as well save the wood," she said. "We'll be warmer in bed anyway."

When she blew out the lamp, the moonlight was shining bright against the window shades, and as we went into the bedroom she raised the shade so we could lie there in bed and watch the full moon rising over the ridge.

We were snug now, Mother and Polly and I, in our white flannel nightgowns, the brick warming our feet. My eyes were just getting heavy when I suddenly heard Mother draw in her breath, felt her hand tighten on my knee.

From outside the window came the faint sound of twigs snapping, of frozen leaves being crunched underfoot.

Mother sat up in bed, clutching the quilt to her throat. I pushed myself up on my elbows, looking toward the window.

The shadow of a man was silhouetted in the moonlight. He was standing only a few feet from the window, turning his head from side to side as he surveyed the house. It must surely have looked deserted, for the fire was banked low and no lamp was lit, though it had been dark only a short time. He began moving around toward the porch.

Mother eased back the covers, put her bare feet down on the linoleum.

I gasped. "Mother, is it . . . ?"

"Sh-h-h," she said. "Sh-h-h. Lie still now."

But Polly and I were both sitting up in bed, our teeth chattering. As Mother started toward the middle room, we slipped out from the quilts and tiptoed behind her.

Now we could hear footsteps moving across the creaking boards of the porch. Mother moved slowly toward the hearth, picked up the poker and edged toward the door. She stood there motionless, like a statue, in her long white gown, her blonde hair streaming over her shoulders, the poker raised.

The doorknob was turning. But the chair held the door closed. The man had not yet put his weight against it.

I tried not to breathe. I looked around for some kind of weapon. The small hearth broom was leaning against the woodbox. I grabbed it and stepped up behind Mother. Polly whimpered.

The sound caused Mother to glance back at us, at me clutching the broom, at Polly whimpering into her hands.

"Oh, my God," she breathed, like beginning a prayer. Then she bent over Polly, whispered, "Hush now, you must hush." She took the broom from my hand and laid both the broom and the poker back down on the hearth. She moved quickly over to the round table and picked up the lamp. The glass chimney rattled as she lifted it off the base and set it on the table. But she didn't strike a match. Not yet. She walked toward the door, and then, with one frenzied motion, she lit the wick, pulled the chair from under the knob, flung open the door.

There on the threshold was the giant shadow, with round, white eyes.

It was wearing a long dark coat, a cap with a bill, and as the glow of the lamp reflected in the white eyes, it might've been something flushed from the woods, caught in the glare of light. But it was a man, his mouth open in terror as if he were looking into a haunted house. There was Mother in the long white gown, holding up a lamp, and behind her were Polly and I shrouded in flannel.

Mother stepped back from the door, shielding the lamp as the flame flickered in the wind. "Come in," she said. "Come in."

His breath rose pale in the night air. His glance passed over the room.

"It's all right," Mother said. "It's only me and . . . me and the girls here."

But he did not move through the door. Only his eyes moved, following Mother as she backed up toward the table, and then turned, setting the lamp down, placing the glass chimney over the wick. The flame became a warm glow now, giving a clear light to the room, and Mother was still visible to the man as she went to the closet, took out her bathrobe. She tied it at the waist and turned again to the dark stranger.

"You must be freezing," she said. "I'll stir up the fire." Her words were measured, her voice neither too loud nor too low.

Slowly, she picked up the poker and stirred the embers, bringing out a flicker of fire.

The man stepped into the room, closing the door behind him. He was dragging his left foot, as if part of him feared to come any farther, but the fire was a trance, holding him, drawing him in. For a moment he stood there blowing on his fingers. And finally he held them out toward the warmth. His hands were gray and cracked. There was moisture in his eyes.

Mother said, "And hungry, too, I'm sure. I'll heat some soup."

As Mother started toward the kitchen, she stopped and looked back at the fire. Already the embers were dying. Soon there'd be nothing but ashes. She looked down at the woodbox, at the one log inside. She leaned over to lift it out.

The man was following her with his eyes, and as she bent over the log, he spoke for the first time, "Let me, Missus."

"Oh no, no! I can . . ."

But he was standing beside her now, and his long arms reached down into the woodbox. He had lifted the log halfway out when his hands suddenly tightened.

Mother caught her lip between her teeth, watching him. Their eyes met. Now it was Mother's eyes that were round, the whites showing, caught by the room's light.

The man's cap shaded his face as he straightened, turned toward the hearth, and placed the log directly over the embers even as the flames licked up against his hand.

Mother said, "I'll only be a minute." To Polly she said, "Come now, you can help me." She put her hand against my cheek. Her fingers were cold. "You set a place at the table."

By the time I'd put the spoon, the plate, and folded the napkin there on the table, Mother was bringing in the soup and the cold biscuits. But the man had sat down on the footstool near the hearth. "This'll do me, Missus," he said.

He sat hunched over, his knees sticking up, as he cradled the bowl of soup in the hollow of his lap. Mother set the plate of biscuits there on the floor beside him, and he took one, chewing with his eyes closed, as if he would shut out everything but the taste of the food. Or maybe, I thought, he wanted to shut out the sight of us, for we were staring at him, hearing him slurping up the soup.

I knew how hard it was to eat soup without slurping, and suddenly my earlier fear of the man changed into my feeling sorry for him, there in the silent room. I said, "Want to hear me sing?"

His mouth was full, and Mother answered for him. "Yes, you do that," she said. "You sing something."

I sang the one about the red, red robin, and brighten the corner where you are. Occasionally I forgot the words, and Mother prompted me while the man continued to eat.

He was scraping his bowl when suddenly we heard the dog in the distance, howling at the moon. The man dropped his spoon.

"That's only the Popes' dog," Mother said. "He howls like that every night."

But the man stood up quickly. "I wouldn't want 'em to find me here," he said. He pulled his cap from his pocket. "It'd be bad on the little'uns."

Mother picked up the plate of biscuits. "Take the rest of them," she said. "You might need them."

He stuffed the biscuits into his pocket and began twisting his cap in his hands. "Missus," he said, fumbling for words, "I didn't aim to scare nobody."

"It's all right," she said.

But he kept twisting his cap, looking down at his hands as if his fingers could spell out the words. "Missus, I'm . . . I'm obliged to you."

"And I to you," she said softly.

He went to the door, leaned out, looking both

ways, and then he ran across the creaking boards of the porch, out into the night.

Mother closed the door and tilted the chair up under the doorknob. But suddenly her body was trembling. The chair fell crashing to the floor. She put her hands to her face, trying to cover her eyes. She was sobbing.

I rarely ever saw her cry, and I watched, helpless, not knowing what to do. Her face was wet, tears dripped from her chin. Her shoulders shook under her long blond hair. Her full robe covered her body, but still I could see the convulsive movements of her chest. Her feet were bare. She'd forgotten to put on her slippers.

I tugged at her sleeve. "Don't cry," I whispered. "Don't be scared."

"But I was, I was." She walked blindly, feeling her way around the chair, across the room. She sank down on the brick hearth, put her head in her hands.

I knelt beside her, tucked her robe up around her feet. "But you weren't scared all the time, were you?" I said. "You weren't scared like Mrs. Pierson, were you?"

She lifted her wet face. "No . . . no, not really like her." She wiped her eyes with the hem of her night-gown. "Mrs. Pierson would've thought only of trying to hurt him. And then he'd have had to hurt her, too. He'd have had no choice then."

I said, "D'you think they'll catch him?"

"I don't know," she sighed. "I just don't know."

We didn't know for several days.

We had told no one that the man had come through Willow Creek. Mother told us that there was goodness in the man, for he could've taken our money if he chose to. Perhaps he'd never had anyone show him any kindness before, she said. She would not betray him, she just couldn't.

So for two days folks made jokes about Mrs. Pierson being holed up in her house, keeping watch for the convict that never appeared.

Then, on Saturday morning, she came into the store, saying that the Lord just never intended that man to pass through these hills.

It happened that a salesman had come into the store that morning, too, and he mentioned casually that the fella who'd escaped from the road gang had been caught trying to cross into Arkansas.

I glanced up at Mother. But folks standing around the stove were eyeing Mrs. Pierson. They grinned.

"Well, he *could've* come through here, like as not!" she said. She sniffed like she could still smell the danger. "And I'm tellin' you right now, if he'd of broken into our house, I'd just never have been the same."

Miss Ada shrugged. "I reckon he'd never have been the same either."

"No, he wouldn't of," Mrs. Pierson said. "We was ready for 'im. We was watchin' and waitin'. At least there was *one* place in these hills where he'd have gotten more'n he ever figured on!" She glanced back over her shoulder. "He'd of found out that *some* folks'll give back the same as they get. And that's the gospel truth!"

Mother smiled at Mrs. Pierson. "Yes, it is," she said. "That's very true."

Mrs. Pierson had been pursing her lips, looking fierce at the other folks. But as Mother spoke, her eyes brightened and she turned toward her.

Mrs. Pierson smiled. Someone was agreeing with her, at last!

7

Miz Pope was a kind, generous woman who believed that the best way to lift the heart is to weight the stomach. Whenever she witnessed trouble or sorrow come on her neighbors, she was hot on its heels, bearing the soup tureen and the fresh bread wrapped in a clean dishcloth.

But then Jim Tomlin came down with the love sickness and hungered only for that thin-waisted city girl. And it caused Miz Pope no end of worry and frustration. It caused her finally to give him the only thing that'd do him any good, and that was a piece of her mind.

"It's not that I got so much I can spare it," she said to Mother, as if it grieved her to have to be harsh with Jim Tomlin. "But that woman's caused him to take leave of his senses. So I've gotta' see he takes mine!"

So that's how we all became involved in what finally happened between Jim and Angie, the girl with the thin waist and the wide smile.

It all began on that early June day when Mother and Polly and I were sitting in Miz Pope's big fragrant kitchen.

She had set us down to plates of strawberry shortcake drenched with thick cream, and then she'd turned back to the window, pulling aside the curtain to get a better view of Jim Tomlin.

The Tomlin place was next to the Popes', separated only by the fence that kept The Mister's turkeys from straying into the Tomlin field.

That field was one of the best in these parts, for here the land broadened out, and the nearby hills sheltered it from the wind, while the creek drained off the heavy rainfall. But it had produced poorly in the early years when old man Tomlin was working it. The old man wasn't much of a farmer, and the elder boys had wanted only to shake the dust from their feet and be gone. So by the time Jim was in his early teens, only he and his aging parents remained on the place.

But it seemed that the land had just been biding its time until Jim was ready for husbandry. Soon as he became tall and strong enough to cultivate the Tomlin farm, it was like the beginning of a love affair. He needed only to lay his hand on the warm, moist earth to know when to plant his cottonseed. He could just walk by a stand of corn, and it'd start to tassel, like a woman fluffing out her hair.

So, through the years, he gave himself only to looking after his land and his aging parents, until, finally, the old folks were laid to rest yonder in the churchyard, and by then Jim was nearing thirty. By then the girls he might've courted were long since married. The younger girls looked on him like a brother. It seemed that Jim would live alone for the rest of his natural days, and Miz Pope was always fretting and stewing about it.

"A man like Jim needs more'n the sound of rain to cause him to turn in his bed," she said that day as she stood at the window watching Jim at work in the field. "But Lord only knows where he'd ever find a woman now." She sighed and pushed back the wisps of hair that clung to her damp forehead. "Can't just any woman live on a farm. I've always said that."

She was to say it again many times in the weeks to come for this was the day when Jim was to find his love, a woman born to sidewalks and paved streets.

This was the day when Miz Pope turned back from the window and stirred her bubbling strawberry jam. And then we heard Jim's truck coming up the lane, pulling around back of the Popes' house.

Miz Pope pulled the coffeepot forward on the wood range just as Jim came through the kitchen door, ducking his head beneath the doorframe.

He was a tall, lean man, built like a bean pole with blue eyes notched in. His face was tanned from the sun, and a blond cowlick touched one side of his forehead.

Miz Pope poured coffee, floated cream on it, but Jim shook his head. "I'm hauling vegetables up for the opening of that hilltop lodge, Miz Pope," he said. "They'll more'n likely pay a good price for eggs today, too, so if you'd like me to carry some up for you . . ."

"Oh, I'd be much obliged!" she said and went hustling out to the henhouse.

I leaned across my plate, whispering to Mother. "Ask him could we go see it."

Few people here had been all the way up to that hilltop to see the lodge. It was part of a new WPA project, the beginning of a state park. But folks here allowed it was just more of the government's tomfoolery. They said Jim Tomlin was plain touched in the head to think it'd ever be a market for his produce. But Jim had gone up to inquire just the same, and he'd come back saying the man running the lodge had promised to buy from him soon's the tourist season opened.

Now Jim walked over to the table, just as if he'd not heard me whispering. "Say, why don't ya'll ride up there with me? We'll all go!"

Mother hesitated, looking at my faded print dress. This was my Saturday dress, plain as bare feet. Tonight Mother would say I looked as if I were made of gingerbread, and she'd start heating water for the washtub. But now she said, "I'm afraid we're hardly presentable, Jim."

But Jim was on my side, and as Miz Pope came back into the kitchen he said, "C'mon, Miz Pope. We're all gonna' ride up yonder and see what the WPA's been doing."

She opened her mouth so wide her gold fillings showed. "Well, aren't we just!" she said. She flung her apron over the chair, hollered out to The Mister that she'd be back 'fore suppertime, and we all crammed into the cab of the truck and went jostling off toward the distant hills.

The road was rutted as it wound over the ridge and on toward the gap, but then we turned onto a fresh blacktop and took the smooth curves leading up to the lodge.

From a distance the windows were gold, as if Midas were among the first tourists. But as we swung around opposite the sun, we saw the lodge was just a rustic, barn-like building. The tourists were wearing outfits that would've made country folks hang their heads.

The men were in overalls with bright patches on the knees, and on their heads were wide straw hats, frayed at the edges. The women wore aprons and sunbonnets, and some even had corncob pipes stuck in their mouths, laughing.

We watched, wide-eyed, such carryings-on, while Mother cautioned us not to point. But after Jim had driven around back and unloaded the truck, he came out saying, "They tell me it's a square dancing jamboree. Let's go watch."

Inside the hall the tourists were congregating while fiddlers took their places on the platform and began tuning up. Then the caller shouted for silence and announced there'd be entertainment from Nashville 'fore the dancing began. He swept off his straw hat and bowed low toward the side door. The girl made her entrance.

She was a slender girl, wearing a white blouse and a pink gingham skirt. Across her shoulders was a wide strap supporting a guitar that appeared too heavy for such a slight girl. And yet, as she moved toward the platform, her walk was graceful, her full skirt swayed rhythmically, as if she'd taken her first steps to music. And though, only a moment before, the caller had been shouting, trying to make himself heard over the tourists' talking and laughing, the girl had only to turn and smile, and a hush came over the hall.

Now in the sudden stillness, we heard Jim Tomlin draw in his breath, as if he'd seen apple blossoms in the middle of winter.

The girl began softly strumming the guitar as she sang of having searched the wide world over for her own true love. Her gaze roamed over the audience as she sang. Finally, she looked toward the back of the hall, toward the place where Jim Tomlin was standing.

He stood nearly a head taller than most men, and as her gaze touched on his tanned face, his blond hair, her hands slowed on the strings, her voice softened to a whisper. Her song ended.

She lowered her head while cheers and applause shook the rafters.

But there was one person who did not applaud— Miz Pope. She was eyeing Jim Tomlin. She was tugging at his sleeve. "We got to get going. We *country folks* got no business here."

But she was speaking to thin air.

Jim was edging his way through the crowd, making a beeline toward the platform and the thinwaisted girl. The girl was coming down from the platform, smiling at the tourists who were clustered around her. The caller was shouting for folks to move back and form their squares. So the way opened up until Jim and the girl stood looking at each other.

She tilted her head back, looking up into his face like a flower turned toward the sun.

Miz Pope was just beside herself. "Lord, wouldn't you just know," she said. "Wouldn't you just know it'd be *that* kind of girl!"

Mother smiled at Miz Pope. "She's a pretty girl."

"Pretty is as pretty does!" she said. "And what could pretty do on a *farm?* Can't you just *see* a fragile little thing like that working on a farm?" She took a deep breath. "C'mon!" And Miz Pope went bustling across the floor toward Jim.

She tugged at his shirt sleeve. "We got to get going." She was tugging at Jim but looking at the girl. "We got to get back to the *farm* where we come from!"

Jim never took his eyes from the girl. "Miz Pope, this is Angie."

Angie smiled at Miz Pope and held out her hand.

For a moment, Miz Pope just stood looking at the small white fingers. Then she stuck out her own rough hand so the girl could touch it. "I'm Jim's neighbor," she said.

But if Angie was taken aback by the dry callouses of the farm woman's hand, she never let on. She said, "I hope ya'll will come again."

"Tourists come here, child," Miz Pope said. "*We* ain't tourists!"

Now the fiddlers were beginning to play, the squares were forming, so Jim had to give in to Miz Pope's tugging at him. He backed away from the girl, not turning his head from her until the dancers closed in and he could no longer see her waving to him.

We rode in silence down the winding road, while Jim swung the truck gentle around the curves, his fingers tapping a rhythmic beat on the steering wheel.

I was sitting on Miz Pope's lap, and I could hear her breath whistling past my ear. Finally she said, "Can't just any woman live on a farm, Jim. You ought to know that."

His profile looked strong in the fading light, but as he turned toward Miz Pope, his eyes foreshadowed sadness. "I do know that, Miz Pope," he said. "I know."

But in the weeks to come, he seemed to know less and less about women and even to forget the very nature of his farm.

All during that summer, Miz Pope kept her vigil at the kitchen window. Each time we were up there, she'd give Mother an eyewitness account.

She reported that the roosters couldn't crow up the sun 'fore Jim was out laboring in his cotton field. He hardly stopped to wipe sweat from his forehead 'less she sent one of her young'uns into the field to carry him a jar of cold buttermilk. But as twilight came on, as dew cooled down the earth, Jim would get in his truck and head for the distant hilltop, for that thin-waisted girl. It was like Jim had two loves, each fighting to claim him from the other.

Miz Pope allowed that Jim was even more handsome as the sun tanned his face and lightened his hair, but she herself was turning gray with worry.

"It's bad enough for him to be courtin' that girl," she said. "But come September that lodge'll be closing up, and suppose then he can't turn loose of that girl. Suppose then he takes it into his head to marry up with 'er. Why, it'd be the ruination of 'im!"

And then came September, and school was out for cotton picking.

It had been a hot, dry summer, and cotton was coming in early. Recently thunderheads had been appearing on the ridge, and folks prophesied that the dry spell would soon end in a gully washer. They'd begun picking cotton dawn to dusk.

"But just look yonder at Jim's cotton," Miz Pope said that day as she looked out her kitchen window.

That day Mother was helping Miz Pope make watermelon pickle. Polly and I were sitting at the table, carving false teeth from watermelon rind.

"He's got the prettiest cotton in these parts," she went on, "but he'll never get it picked 'fore the rain comes. He should've known he'd have to hire extra hands this year, but now they're all spoken for. And it's 'cause he's had nothing but that girl on his mind. *Now* you see how the misery's come on 'im!"

It had, too. Normally you could see Jim out in his fields, striding along with the sun full on his face, the dust puffing up like a cloud beneath his feet. But today he was just staring down at his cotton, his hands hanging slack at his sides while the sun made hollow shadows on his cheeks.

Miz Pope stood there grieving over the sight of Jim until finally she said, "Well, I got to give 'im a piece of my mind."

She went out the back door and hollered across to Jim that she had something for him. Then she came back in, wiped the watermelon seeds from the oil-cloth, and set him a place with pie and coffee.

As he came into the kitchen, he forgot to duck under the door. He banged his forehead but didn't even flinch, as if he didn't feel it. He sat down at the table but never lifted his fork, as if his mouth didn't water at the sight of Miz Pope's pie.

She was watching him. She sighed. "Now, Jim, I don't aim to be a know-it-all. But I know, sure as this world, that farm life's hard on women not born to it. It can make them mighty miserable. Make their man miserable, too."

"I've been studying about going up to Nashville," Jim said, "about lookin' for work up there."

Miz Pope threw up her hands. "Doing *what*, for lands sake? Selling nails in a hardware store?"

Jim didn't answer.

Miz Pope was shaking her head from side to side like she was sifting through her mind for the right words. Then she nodded, having found what she was looking for. "I wonder could you spare me your truck this afternoon?" she said. "I've got need for it."

Jim rose. "Sure. I'll bring it 'round."

His pie was still untouched, but Miz Pope let him go. "I told him true," she said to Mother. "I've got need to see that girl!"

Mother shook her head. "Oh, I wouldn't if I were you."

"If you was me," Miz Pope said, "then you'd do what I'm doing." And she persuaded Mother that we should ride up there with her.

As Miz Pope hunched over the wheel and let out the clutch, the truck rared like an ornery mule. But soon we were loping over the ridge, hightailin' it up the black road toward the hilltop lodge.

We were nearing the rustic building when we caught sight of Angie, sitting alone on a tree stump alongside the lodge. She was gazing off toward the hills that embraced Jim's land. And as Miz Pope slowed the truck, Angie glanced back, recognized the truck, and came running toward it, smiling into the sun.

Then she recognized Miz Pope at the wheel. She frowned, shading her eyes with her hand as she looked up into the cab. "Where's Jim?"

"He's where he belongs!" Miz Pope said. But then as she saw how the girl's shoulders drooped, how her small white hand fell to her side, Miz Pope sighed as if some of the steam had gone out of her. "It's just that he belongs on his land, girl. Just like you belong in the city."

Angie smiled. "I'm really from Clinton. That's only a one-horse town, Miz Pope."

"Well, that's one more horse'n you'll see working a farm," she said. Then she leaned out the window, looked down at Angie, and explained how it takes a strong mule to work the rocky soil around Willow Creek. She told how Jim had labored to bring in his cotton, and now he was in danger of losing it 'cause of having worried about losing Angie. "So if you'll just get on back to the city and make it clear he's not to follow you," she said, "then maybe he'll be able to tend his land, to bring in his cotton 'fore it's plain ruined."

Tears were forming in Angie's eyes, but still she smiled at Miz Pope. Even with the sun and the tears blinding her, she smiled. "I'm glad you told me," she said. "Thank you for coming."

Miz Pope sighed, "Well, I reckon I'll be a-thankin' you for *going*."

Then she put the truck in reverse, and we backed around, and headed toward Willow Creek where we belonged.

It was late the next afternoon before we saw Miz Pope again.

Mother and Polly and I were at home, sitting out on the porch shelling peas, when we saw Miz Pope come hustling up the path toward our house. She started calling out to us soon as she came within shouting distance. "Ya'll got to come see what's happening! C'mon. You'll never believe your eyes!"

"What? What is it?" Mother stood up so quickly the peas rolled from her lap.

But Miz Pope just shooed us on up the road, not giving away her secret until we neared Jim Tomlin's cotton field.

Then we saw the cars parked on both sides of the road. We saw the tourists wearing their straw hats and their gingham bonnets, swarming up and down the furrows of Jim's field.

And there was Angie, sitting up on the cotton

wagon, singing and playing her guitar while the
tourists laughed and picked the cotton.

Jim was emptying the sacks into the wagon bed,
pausing only to boost young 'uns up onto the seat beside Angie so they could get their pictures taken.
Then he'd throw back his head and laugh, like there
was a happiness inside him had to burst out.

Miz Pope was shaking her head. "She's made it a
jamboree," she said, "a real jamboree!"

Suddenly Angie looked up from her playing and
caught sight of us standing there alongside the
fence. She lifted her hand from the guitar just long
enough to wave and smile at Miz Pope.

Miz Pope glanced sideways at Mother. "Well, it's
like I said—not just any woman can live on a farm!"

Then she grinned and waved back at Angie. "But a
woman with a smile and a song carries happiness
with her," she said, "and I reckon she can live any-
where."

8

Along toward morning, it began to rain.

It came from off there in the hills with a muffled roll of thunder, and then the curtains stirred, pale, ghost-like as the cloud moved in closer. A shimmer of lightning reflected itself in the mirror, a breath of wind set the chairs to rocking outside on the porch, and finally the slow spring rain dripped softly from the trees, like a pretty woman crying.

Dawn took its own sweet time easing down from the ridge that Sunday morning, while the birds twittered nervously and the roosters crowed off and on, arguing among themselves about the time.

I had been awakened by that thunder, had lain on a pallet, listening, as the cloud came closer into the hills.

Emily Long was spending the night with us, sharing the bed with Mother. So I lay quietly on the pallet beside Polly until finally Mother and Emily got up and went out to the kitchen. I waited until I heard the sizzle of salt pork in the iron skillet, smelled the coffee perking, and then I got up and ran into the kitchen just as if I were going about my usual chores of wiping the oilcloth, setting the table, not letting on that I was anxious to see what Emily Long was doing.

Emily was standing by the window, gazing out through the curtains. Her dark hair, curled last night with the curling iron, tumbled around her shoulders. Her blue flannel bathrobe, tied loosely at the waist, made her body look soft and warm. And now as she turned, taking the cup of coffee Mother held out to her, I saw that there was still a glow in her dark eyes, a flush on her cheeks, and I sighed with relief.

Folks here in Willow Creek were right fond of Emily, but they'd never taken her to be a pretty woman. Not until lately. But lately, there'd been a change come over Emily. Folks had witnessed a soft glow in her eyes. They'd seen her thin body take on a swan-like grace. And they'd known for true. Emily had been kissed.

Now she turned back to the window, lifted the white veil of curtain from the glass, and gazed out toward the hills. "But it *is* a strange cloud," she said.

The long gray cloud was drifting, like a restless spirit, alongside the ridge. The rain was tapping against the windowpane.

"Oh, but it's early yet," Mother said, taking biscuits from the oven. "The sun'll come out. You'll see."

This kind of talk was sure to be repeated throughout the community that morning as folks rose and took notice of that cloud. They set great store by the dark or light of the moon, by whether or not the sun shone on the day of a wedding.

This was the day of Emily's wedding to Chet Daniels. And though some folks had agreed with Mrs. Pierson when she said the Lord never intended that wedding, there wasn't a living soul who'd miss it.

A wedding Sunday usually meant that the church would be packed to the rafters, for preaching would be cut short and there'd be no calling for sinners to come forward during the closing hymn. There'd be just the Amen, and then Angie Tomlin would strike a chord on the piano and begin the wedding march.

Normally the chancel would be bright with flowers, and there outside the church windows the cemetery would be decorated, too, for folks brought blossoms arranged in Mason jars and set them on the graves of the departed. Afterwards, the weather allowing, folks would linger around outside, while the children chased among the headstones (being careful not to step across a grave) and the grown-ups talked of crops and babies.

But there'd never been a wedding quite like this one, and on this Sunday morning folks would be casting their eyes toward that cloud and wondering if it was something to be reckoned with; worrying that it was a bad omen.

It's no wonder that Emily Long was worrying too.

Emily had been in love with Chet Daniels for nearly two years, ever since he'd come here. But Mother was the only one who suspected it, at first. Certainly Chet didn't.

Whenever Chet came into the store, Emily would just blush and busy herself over the charge books. And just as Mother had predicted, a girl who knew how to look sidelong at a man had latched onto Chet. Emily had not learned in time. The only thing Emily *had* learned was to buy herself a pretty dress once in a while and force Bubba to raise pigs and buy his own tobacco.

Emily also stopped by occasionally to sit and visit with Mother, and they'd become close friends. When, finally, Emily got a second chance at having Chet for her very own, Mother had done everything to encourage her. And when folks began whispering about the wedding, Mother was the only one who didn't act skittish at the thought. She'd even suggested that Emily bring over the new spring catalogue and together they could select the bride's dress.

Emily had come several weeks ago, bringing the catalogue, but she hadn't opened it right away. She'd sat for a while, gazing into the fire, saying,

"Now it mustn't look anything like . . . ," she took a deep breath, "nothing at all like . . ."

"No, not like Maribeth's," Mother said, as if there were nothing fearful in the name.

As she voiced Maribeth's name, she seemed to dispel the fear in Emily, too. She opened the catalogue, turned the pages past the white wedding dresses. Finally, they selected a yellow voile with a ribbon sash and full sleeves. Later, Mother took some lace from the trunk she kept pushed under the bed and made a ruffled hat for the bride.

Now it was Sunday morning and Mother touched Emily's shoulder, easing her into a chair at the table.

"Oh, you'll be a lovely bride," she said, glancing toward the yellow dress.

Emily had brought the dress down last night, and after they'd curled Emily's hair with the curling iron, they'd ironed the dress and suspended it on a hanger between the doorway, where it swayed now in the warm, kitchen air.

"Why, you'll be the prettiest bride ever . . ." Mother began.

Emily's head jerked up; her mouth quivered. Then she lowered her head, gazed into her coffee cup.

"Now Emily . . . Emily . . . ," Mother said. She eased herself into her chair, put her hand over Emily's. The two of them just sat there, their heads bowed over the coffee cups as if they were observing a moment of silence.

I was surprised at Mother letting those words slip out, because she'd cautioned us before Emily came to say nothing today that could upset her. But I guess it was bound to happen, sooner or later. The memory of Maribeth Wilson was just bound to manifest itself whenever mention was made of the prettiest bride ever seen in the Community Church.

Folks always spoke of Maribeth as "the bride," though in truth she never was. She was dressed in the long white gown, all right, and the lace veil was arranged over her pale, beautiful face. But she was dead.

On the day she was supposed to marry Chet Daniels, the most marriageable man in these hills, she was laid out in her wedding dress there in the Community Church. On the day she would've been smiling and nodding her golden head, she was lowered beneath a headstone there in the churchyard.

The headstone was weathering now, and the rosebushes planted alongside had a year's growth on them. But talk had arisen the day Maribeth died, and it had grown into a legend that lived on.

The legend began naturally enough, like a seed that falls on fertile soil.

It began a year ago during the early spring when

the earth was too wet for the plow, when hens were still settin' their nests, and folks had time to gather at the store where talk ripened in the warmth of the stove. They talked, in the beginning, of how Maribeth had looked, a sleeping beauty, lying there in her wedding dress. They spoke of how Miz Wilson had stood beside her casket, wearing the black hat set straight on her head, her dark eyes dry as glass as she looked on the faces of those who filed silently by the chancel.

And then folks would pause, and take in their breath, ready now to speak of the strange thing that had come over Chet Daniels. They had seen his skin become the color of ashes, his flesh melting from his bones, and his eyes become those of a man haunted.

Then they'd shiver like with a chill coming on, and they'd wait until somebody opened the stove's belly and fed it split pine.

"It was a day of reckoning," they'd say, warming again, "for man and woman alike."

The man was Chet Daniels, an outsider, having been here just long enough to bring in one crop before the terrible thing happened. But this time when the curse came on the man who owned the old McFarland place they didn't blame the willow. Chet had cut down the willow—even dug out the roots—because, he said, they were getting into his cistern. So this time they blamed the man himself.

He'd never told much about himself except that

he'd grown up at the institute near Nashville, which everybody knew was a place for boys with no folks. He *had* told the farmers some new-fangled ways about farming, but they were strange ways, having nothing to do with the dark or light of the moon. And even during that bad drought he'd wasted his sweat trying to dig deeper into his well, and never once did he hang a snake—belly side up—on his fence. The other farmers did, and finally brought rain. But they sure got no help from Daniels.

But now he was seeing that they'd told him true. There were things to be reckoned with that never came from a book.

The woman was Miz Wilson, who'd used a charm falsely and seen it turn back on 'er.

The Wilsons had lived in these hills since time began, and she, like her mother and grandmother before her, had always been called on for birthings, for mixing herb tonics, for curing warts and styes. But folks never considered this conjuring. And perhaps, in truth, it wasn't.

Doctors will tell you, right today, that warts are cussed things that'll disappear for unaccountable reasons, and a gold ring rubbed over the lid does give off a kind of oxide.

So folks never reckoned on Miz Wilson having the power to put a curse on you. But now they'd seen it come on Chet Daniels, and they stood around the stove and wondered on it.

Now there were women who remembered back to

the time before Maribeth was even born, and they came forward and testified to their remembering.

So the legend had taken root, and now it began to grow.

Miz Wilson, they said, had been getting on toward middle age when she'd first felt a quickening in her womb, and knew, at last, that the herb tonic had taken hold. She told that a woman of her years was more'n likely to have a girl-child, and she took to eating honey from beehives in the peach orchard, to reading Psalms morning and night, and she never once raised her voice to her husband, though he was never much 'count and in time left her and the little 'un and went off to Cincinnati, Ohio.

They remembered that she'd carried the baby longer than usual and, when she finally delivered herself, the child was all filled out, with dimples and blonde curls. There were some who reasoned that the baby had filled out in the womb, but even that couldn't explain how a dark-eyed bony woman could produce that blonde child.

Maribeth grew, so the story went, like something charmed. Her eyes were blue as evening sky. Her hair was a silken tassel, and her body ripened with the seasons.

Maribeth was eighteen that spring when Chet Daniels came to these hills and bought the old McFarland place. He bought it for next to nothing, but no one else had shown any interest in it, and

McFarland was tickled to get anything a'tall. But Chet had known how to spray those black-limbed apple trees, to plant kudzu on the worn hills, and you could tell he'd make that place amount to something.

Well, naturally the women in the community started perking up. They even spent egg money on Sunday-meeting dresses for their daughters.

But it seemed that all Miz Wilson had to do was crook her finger and Chet would follow her and Maribeth home for Sunday dinner.

'Course, they allowed that she'd taught Maribeth something about charming too.

Maribeth had always had a way of looking at boys that'd drive 'em wild as March hares. But now it was as if she'd just been practicing, just waitin' until Chet Daniels came along, and then she took him as if he were her birthright.

It was during the dead of winter that Miz Wilson came into the store and asked Emily Long to order her some white dimity, some wide lace. Emily had taken the pencil from behind her ear and slowly written the order. But the women standing there were quick to turn sour-looking. And when Miz Wilson cackled out, "Gonna' be a wedding!" they knew she spoke true.

They had passed the old McFarland place, had looked up there, and had seen Chet Daniels nailing shingles on the roof, bricking up the chimney, working like a man possessed.

But it was one of those hard winters when the long freeze gives way to heavy rains and you patch one thing only to find another gone bad.

Now the road leading up into Chet's place was pocked with holes, gnawed by gullies, and they'd heard him worrying that his truck was worn thin from hauling over it.

They knew for sure that he had a worried mind on the day he came into the store and asked Emily Long to order secondhand tires from the salesman on his next trip through.

So Emily had ordered them, and the tires were there, propped against the feed sacks, on that Friday before the wedding when Chet and Maribeth came in.

Mother and Polly and I had stopped by the store from school that afternoon, since Mother was intending to pay her bill. But Emily had suggested that Mother wait until tomorrow when Miss Ada would be there to give us candy. So we'd gone on home, and there were only a few folks to witness what happened in the store that drizzling afternoon in March. But those few told the story over and over 'til it all became so clear in the mind's eye that you could see it all happen, start to finish. You could hear every word.

The moment Chet and Maribeth came in you could see they didn't look like a couple about to set up housekeeping. Her mouth was in a pout, his neck red around the collar.

He went striding over to Emily. "Tell the salesman he'll have to take back those tires." He spoke loud, as if he were really shouting at Maribeth. "I got no way of paying 'til I bring in a crop. I'll make do 'til then."

Maribeth stuck out that pink lower lip. "And 'til you're willing to bring in my spool bed, and my dresser, and the cheval mirror ma's giving me . . ."

He rooted his feet. "I'm not hauling over that road today," he said, mule-like. "Nothing's gonna' make me."

She gave him the sheep's eye. She put her soft hand on his shoulder. "Well, if you want me to go to that old McFarland place without nice things . . ."

She turned and went sashaying out of the store with him following.

The last folks saw, they were climbing into the empty truck, heading off toward the Wilsons'.

An hour had passed when Chet was spotted coming around the bend of the road. He was on foot and carrying something, and at first you couldn't make it out. Then he came on past the stand of cottonwoods, and folks saw and went a-running.

He was carrying Maribeth. Her body dangled limp in his arms. Her golden hair swung back and forth as he walked.

132

Folks went running, hollering "Lord save us!" and then, "She's gone . . . my Lord, she's gone!"

Later, when men went to pull the truck from the gully just past the gate of the old McFarland place, they saw that the bald tire had blown, split wide open, and that the spool bed was broken, the mirror splintered, scattered through the mud.

Chet had gotten a deep gash on his face, but Maribeth never got a scratch. Just one blow to the head, and not a scratch on 'er. But she was dead just the same.

The men tried to take her from Chet, but he just kept walking on past the store, staring straight ahead, on down the road and up the hill, carrying Maribeth back to her ma. His mouth was open, his breath rasping in his throat, but he said not a word, like he'd turned dumb.

One of the men ran ahead to tell Miz Wilson about the accident, for they could see her standing out by her picket fence, squinting down toward that strange procession.

At first, she just moaned and shut her eyes as if to make the sight disappear. Then, as they neared the gate, she ran out, calling to Maribeth, trying to call her back.

Chet carried the girl on into the house and laid her on the thick hooked rug by the fire. Then he just stood, his arms hanging slack, empty.

Miz Wilson knelt down, crooning, speaking like

in an unknown tongue while the men watched, not knowing what was to come. Then, there in the firelight, Miz Wilson looked up. Her eyes were like burning coals. And that's when she looked on Chet Daniels.

Suddenly, a shiver passed over him. The breath was drawn from his body. His shoulders slumped as if unseen blows were being rained on him. The curse had already begun to eat into his flesh.

Maribeth was buried that first Sunday in March, buried in her wedding dress, while clouds shrouded the hills, drizzled on the trees. Everyone in Willow Creek went to that funeral. We went, too. But after the service, when folks began lining up to view the body, Mother asked Jim Tomlin if he'd drop us by home as he took Angie. Angie was in a family way now and was feeling a little faint.

All through March, clouds shrouded these hills. Even into April there was a soft weeping through the trees. And now folks at the store began whispering that Miz Wilson had surely put a curse on us all. Plows were miring up in the fields, and a wet spring was a sure sign that boll weevils would plague the cotton.

The men said it plain wasn't right that they be held accountable, for they'd have let Chet use their wagons for hauling, had they thought on it. And the women said that, in truth, they'd never thought bad of Maribeth for charming Chet Daniels away from the other girls.

Mother always tried to avoid these conversations at the store. She'd go there only to get a sack of sugar, a can of coal oil. But while she talked with Emily, Polly and I would move nearer the stove, listening, 'til Mother pulled us back, handed us a sack, and told us to make ourselves useful.

Folks were inclined to lower their voices then, for they still considered "that Wasson lady" an outsider who believed only the things written in books. There's no telling what they'd have done had they known about the time we actually went up to Miz Wilson's house.

It was about a month after the funeral, on the first Saturday without rain, when Mother got out our coats and said, "We're going up to call on Mrs. Wilson."

I pulled back. "Not me. I'm 'fraid of her!" I'd heard the kids at school say they'd seen Miz Wilson walking in the graveyard, and only the big boys would take a dare to cut across her place on the way home.

Mother buttoned me into my coat. "Nonsense!"

It was a long walk, but Mother pointed out the robins nesting, the trees stretching their limbs to the sun, and I forgot to be afraid until we saw the dark cedars there in the churchyard and the path leading up toward the picket fence.

I shivered at the sight of that clothesline stretched

out back of the house, at that row of black dresses writhing in the wind. I'd heard at school that Miz Wilson dipped her dresses into that big black kettle out back and hung 'em out to scare you.

But now Mother was knocking at the door, and Miz Wilson opened it, just as if she'd been standing there all the time, watching us come.

"Good afternoon," Mother said. "How are you, Mrs. Wilson?"

"I'm fit," she said. "You?" She squinted at us, as if considering which one would get the poultice.

"Fine," Mother said. "We just stopped by."

Miz Wilson motioned us into the dim room. The shades were half drawn, the room hot and close, the windows sweating.

"We interrupt your supper?" Mother asked. It was only the middle of the afternoon, but I reckoned she was wondering about that pot bubbling on the stove.

"I've no set time," she said. "It's Brunswick stew . . . more'n plenty for me." Without asking, she went to the stove, ladled the liquid into bowls, and set them on the table. "You'll like it," she said, looking straight at me.

It was hard to swallow with that picture of Maribeth looking down from the mantel, but Mother was looking at me, too. So I ate, and for days afterward I silently watched my hands for warts, wondering if I'd be turned into a toad.

Finally, I decided Mother had kept the hex away

because she didn't fear it. Or maybe the hex was just too busy working on Chet Daniels.

As spring gave in to summer his face became tanned, but that only made the scar whiter on his cheek, his eyes more feverish.

On Sundays he'd stand outside the church, waiting for Miz Wilson to appear. She always wore the black dress, the black hat set straight on her head, and her dark eyes were dry as glass. Folks had never seen a tear shed from her eyes, but they did see the way Chet followed her into her pew, moving with heavy feet as if he were being pulled by unseen forces. They saw, too, that she beckoned him home for Sunday dinner and that his bones could not take on flesh.

Now that the ground had dried out, there were the usual church dinners where long tables were set up alongside the cemetery and women brought in bountiful platters. It used to be that Miz Wilson's Brunswick stew was as welcome as Miz Pope's pie, but now as folks watched Chet eat of her concoction they shied away, leaving it to grow cold.

That summer Chet was a marriageable man again, but not a man free. If any girl looked sidelong at him, her ma would yank 'er back, hurry 'er away.

But Emily Long had no ma to look out for her. She never actually looked sidelong at Chet anyway. The only thing she did was ask the salesman to let Chet try out that new hybrid corn he was peddling.

The corn grew tall, and even Chet stood straighter when he brought in those fine roasting ears. Then Emily saw to it that Chet got samples of some new-fangled fertilizer that had been sent to the store, and in the fall, when he brought in his apple crop, he brought Emily a crate of the finest ones, in a manner of thanking. Emily made him some applesauce to show she was much obliged. But of course no one even suspected that those two were taking an interest in each other.

But Mother knew that when the maples turned gold, when the creek was singing softly in its bed, Chet and Emily fished it together. And as the hickory nuts began falling from the trees, they walked in the woods, gathering them.

Emily brought us a sack of the cracked nuts one Sunday afternoon, and she and Mother sat there by the fire, shelling, talking.

"I just wish I could make it all up to him," Emily said. She tossed the hulls into the fire, watched them blaze. "That day last spring . . . ," she said, "That day, I should've told him to take those tires on account, and I didn't. I didn't say a word."

Mother looked exasperated. "Now, Emily, you know Miss Ada never allows you to give anyone that much credit without her say-so. You've got to quit worrying about that. You and Chet both must quit dwelling in the past." She looked down at her hands, turning her gold band. "Be happy now with loving him."

Emily blushed. "Well I . . . I've always had a liking for him," she said softly.

Through the long, bleak winter, their liking for each other deepened until, finally, they began sitting together in church. Emily and Chet and Miz Wilson.

Miz Wilson would go first into the pew, and then Emily, then Chet. So now Emily was sitting between those two, as if her body could shield her beloved. But Emily had the wide, frightened look of a doe.

She had heard folks talking. "Well, *I* wouldn't want to be the one . . . ," they said. "I wouldn't want any daughter of *mine* . . ."

And now it was more'n a year since Maribeth was lowered into the ground. And it was Emily's wedding day. And there was the long gray cloud drifting over the hills. There was rain weeping through the cottonwoods while Emily sat in our kitchen, staring into her coffee cup.

Mother said, "There's certainly nothing unusual about a spring rain, Emily!"

Emily looked up. "Unless it's a sign . . ."

"A sign of spring!" Mother said. "And so's a robin."

Emily smiled then, as if relieved to let her happiness show. And by the time she'd lifted the yellow dress over her head, tucked her dark hair under the lace cap, she was beautiful.

Now we heard the Popes' car braking beside

our porch. The Mister had recently gotten a Model T, and Miz Pope had said they'd be proud to ride us to the church. She said we mustn't risk having Chet come and see the bride before the wedding.

Miz Pope came bustling in, exclaiming over Emily, pretty as could be. "But where's your flowers?" she said.

Emily glanced at Mother. Emily and Chet had decided not to decorate the chancel and just to have a simple marrying, to show their respect. But Miz Wilson had said she wanted to cut the bride's bouquet from her garden, and Chet felt it best to let her, but folks didn't need to know.

Mother spoke up. "They'll be at the church, Miz Pope."

But as it turned out, folks did know who cut the flowers.

They saw Emily standing there at the chancel, holding the yellow roses mixed with blue iris, trailing wisteria. And as she promised to love and cherish, for better, for worse, folks glanced at Miz Wilson sitting there all in black. They followed her gaze out the church window, out into the mist of the cemetery, and then they saw the roses, the iris, the trailing wisteria set there in the Mason jar, set there as if they were being held up by something beneath the earth.

Folks looked around, whispering to each other.

Then the preacher was lifting his hands, giving

the Amen. The congregation chimed in, echoing "Amen!"

But in that church there wasn't a living soul who really believed they'd seen the end of this.

No one saw much of the newlyweds during the next month. It was a busy time now for farmers, and for Mother, too. She was expecting a visit from the County Superintendent and was readying her reports.

Emily had stopped by to bring us a frying chicken, but she couldn't visit long. She was helping Chet put underpinning around the house, she said, 'cause there was always a draft creeping over the floor. She frowned when she said it, but she was smiling, waving, as she left.

Then school was out for cotton chopping that June day when we saw Chet come into the store.

Mother had given Polly and me each a penny, and we were standing at the counter trying to decide between horehound and licorice.

Mother walked over to Chet. She smiled. "And how's your sweet bride?"

"Oh . . . well now, she's . . ." he hesitated. Folks turned, listening. "She's had a little spell."

Mother motioned us to take the horehound and come on. "We'll ride back with you," she said.

We climbed into his truck and started on down the road.

"It's not bad, is it?" Mother said.

"Well, Emily says not. But I dunno."

Mother looked worried as we turned off the main road. We were pulling up the lane when suddenly Chet braked the truck so hard we rocked forward. Mother gave us a glance of inspection, but only Chet appeared to be hurt.

His forehead was streaked with sweat. His breath was a hoarse rasp. His hands gripped the wheel so hard the veins rose like twisted cord.

"Look!" he cried, pointing toward the gully. "It keeps coming back . . . you *see* it?"

There was something shining there, like a piece of broken mirror that caught the sun and threw it back on the windshield.

Mother let out her breath. "Of course I see it. I'm always seeing things in ditches . . . pieces of tin, bits of glass."

He turned his tormented face to Mother. "You don't see it for what it is," he said. "You weren't born to these hills."

"I wasn't born a fool!" she said. But as Chet started up again, she leaned over as if moving away from the gearshift and looked back down into that gully.

When we drove into the yard, we saw Emily standing there on the porch. Mother hurried up to her. "Honey, are you all right?"

"It comes and goes," Emily said. Then her cheeks flushed, and she leaned nearer Mother, whispering, "I didn't aim to tell 'til I start showing . . ."

Mother let out her breath. "Oh, Emily, I'm *so* glad for you." She hesitated. "But it's such happy news, maybe it *should* be told now. Maybe you'd let *me* tell, all right?"

So when Chet took us home that afternoon, Mother asked him to let us off at the store.

By the next day, everyone knew.

Women started going to see Emily, telling her she must start eating for two, telling her to have Miz Pope for the birthing as other women were doing. These days, they were fearful of having Miz Wilson look on a newborn child.

Miz Wilson did go to see Emily, though, soon as she heard she was in a family way. She took Emily an angel cake, told her she'd have a girl-child. She told it at the store, too, said she knew by the way Emily was carrying it.

Miz Wilson bought pink yarn from Miss Ada and began crocheting. It was, folks said, as if she was expecting Maribeth to come back. So women bought the blue yarn, and crocheted caps and bootees as if, by sheer number, they could outwit her.

But Emily bought the pink. She was making a bonnet the day she came by to sit with Mother.

Emily's arms had stayed thin, but her stomach and her eyes were enormous. She said that Chet was taking her in to Town, where she'd stay with her second cousin and have her baby in a hospital.

Emily left Willow Creek two weeks before the

baby was due, and she stayed away until the little girl was a month old. Everybody kept wondering what the child would look like, but when Emily came back, it was Mother who saw her first.

Chet came for us that winter afternoon, said Emily was home and wanted us to come.

We scrambled into the truck as Mother asked how they were and Chet said they were just fine. As we were nearing the lane, Mother said, "You never did say what you've named the baby."

But Chet was getting down to open the gate, and now he walked to the edge of the gully and stood staring down into it. The winter sun was pale, and there were only shadows in the ditch, and finally he got back into the truck.

Emily was sitting by the fire, holding the baby wrapped in a pink crocheted blanket. The baby opened her eyes as Mother picked her up and said, "Oh, Emily, she's just like you!"

Emily smiled. "Oh no, not like me. She's beautiful."

She was, I thought, sort of funny looking. Her dark hair grew in straight tufts, and her eyes were all squinted up as she waved her tiny fists.

Emily said, "We're going to baptize her on Sunday, name her Maribeth."

Mother sank into the rocker. "Oh, Emily . . . *must* you?"

Emily nodded. "Chet feels that we . . . that we owe it to Miz Wilson, you see?"

Mother looked at Chet for a long moment. "I wonder if I do," she said.

Mother let us touch the tiny fists, have some of Emily's tea cakes, before she looked again at Chet. "We really must go."

But we didn't go far, as it turned out. We rode only as far as the gate before Mother turned to Chet. "This is quite far enough."

She spoke quietly, but there was a tremor in her voice like a lull before the storm. Then, her voice rising, she said, "I wouldn't *dare* ride on with you!"

Her hands were shaking as she reached over me, opened the door, hustled us down from the running board, and then she was shouting up at Chet. "There's a *curse* on you, Chet Daniels!"

He came running around the front of the truck. Sweat was streaking his face. "Then you *did* see it!" he cried. "You saw it all along!"

"Yes! Yes, I saw it! But I didn't know what it was. I didn't see that you'd put a curse on *yourself!* Oh, but I see it now, plain as day. Every time you passed this gully, every time Miz Wilson looked at you, you cursed yourself, damning yourself with guilt for something you couldn't have helped!"

She gasped for breath and went on.

"And then you showed folks what a curse *really* is, and scared 'em out of their senses! All because there was first an accident and then a few natural happenings which were taken to be *unnatural* signs!"

She put her hands on her hips. "But you can't rid

yourself of it, can you? And you'll keep right on 'til you've pulled Emily down with you, 'til the sins of the father are visited on his children, from generation to generation!"

She fumbled for a handkerchief, blew her nose. "But you are right about one thing. You *do* owe something to Mrs. Wilson! You owe that lonely, grief-stricken old woman some solace, some compassion. *She* can't work magic, Chet Daniels, but maybe you can. So start conjuring!"

She turned, grabbing our hands, running on toward the road.

I glanced back once, and Chet was just standing there beside the gully, staring after us.

On Sunday, church began in the usual way with the singing, the preaching, and then, during the final hymn, we felt a rush of air as the back door opened and Chet and Emily came in.

Emily was wearing a new yellow dress, and she was smiling as women always did when they brought their firstborn in for baptizing.

They walked straight down the aisle until they paused at the pew where Miz Wilson was sitting. Chet leaned over and touched her arm. She looked up at him and rose, as if knowing he was coming.

The three of them walked up to the chancel, and then Chet placed the baby in Miz Wilson's arms, just as if he had no fear of her looking on it.

There was a breathless hush in the church as the preacher said, "Name the baby."

Chet's voice rang out. "Her name is Emilene Long Daniels."

The preacher sprinkled water on Emilene's head, and then slowly they turned to face the congregation. Suddenly, Miz Wilson started to cry. So now Emily took the baby, and Chet took Miz Wilson into his arms right there in front of everybody, and he held her close while she cried on his shoulder and the straight black hat tumbled from her head.

Folks started moving up, slowly at first, to see the baby. But then the women were crying and clasping Miz Wilson to their bosoms, while the men pumped Chet's hand.

So now the legend had come full circle. The curse was falling from Chet's shoulders. Miz Wilson was being changed back into a plain, dark-eyed woman. And a ghost was laid to rest.

There in the hills, folks told of the strange thing they'd witnessed that day. They said it was like something akin to magic. And they spoke true.

They'd seen a sign of love.

9

During the season when the hills were bedded down under dry leaves and plows hibernated inside the barns, folks were inclined to sit around the store and just *talk* about the weather. But when the roosters began crowing up the early dawn, when the earth could be crumbled like warm cornbread in the hand, then it was time to straighten up the lightning rods and attempt to placate the heavens.

Those who had known many seasons in these hills had seen the time when spring came softly, waking the earth with a gentle touch of rain. But they also bore witness to the time spring came roaring into the hills, lashing out with wind and lightning.

It had been some years now since that fierce day when cattle were struck down in the fields, when trees were snatched up by the roots. That had occurred before Mother and Polly and I came to Willow Creek, but we'd often heard folks talk of the day they'd been blown nearly to Kingdom Come. We'd seen children rolling their eyes whenever thunder began growling in the belly of the earth.

Always when spring came, lightning rods were the first things to sprout. Miss Ada ordered them even as she ordered seed, and farmers would add still another tall steel pole to their roofs, as if an approaching storm could know its forces were outnumbered.

Some of the houses had root cellars off the kitchen, and families would hustle down those steps whenever a thunderhead rose up in the west. But Mrs. Pierson vowed the Lord never intended you should get down underneath a house where it could collapse, burying you alive. She had an honest-to-goodness storm shelter dug into the hill behind their house, and on February 2 she'd be watching the heavens, wondering if the sun would come out, if the groundhog would see his shadow. If he did, he'd burrow right back into the earth, and we'd have six more weeks of winter. But if he didn't, then spring was a-comin', storm clouds would soon be threatening, and Mrs. Pierson would begin readying the shelter.

She'd make Billy Bob knock down those spider webs from the wooden supports while she swept the hard dirt floor, filled the lamp, and began her vigil.

But until that Friday in March, Mother and Polly and I had never experienced a cloud that brought anything worse than a roll of thunder, a quiver of lightning. So Mother was not concerned that we had no root cellar, no lightning rods. Even when Billy Bob was sent down to say, "Grandma says it's clabbering up. Ya'll better come a-runnin'!" Mother usually just thanked him. She'd take a quick glance at the sky, and tell him we'd better stay home in case we'd need to get our wash in off the line.

After he'd gone, Mother would shake her head. "I never saw a woman could make so much of a little clabber."

So Polly and I were not afraid of spring. To us, it was a time when we could shed our long underwear and squish our bare toes in the warm mud puddles left from the rain. And though we'd gone a few times to the dark tomb of Mrs. Pierson's shelter, it was only because Polly and I looked on it as an adventure. It was only because we had pulled at Mother's skirt until she agreed to go. Then we'd go running up the hill, hollering to Billy Bob that we were coming, to save us a place.

Space in the shelter was limited, so Mrs. Pierson was particular about whom she invited to come and be saved. So we felt glorified to be among the chosen, to go running up the hill and see Mrs. Pierson standing there, glancing up at the heavens, like Noah waiting to load the Ark. Then she'd beckon us inside and signal to Billy Bob to bolt the door behind us.

There, inside, the women would sit on wooden boxes, exchanging gossip, while the men sat near the lamp, repairing harnesses. Sometimes Angie would be there with her guitar, answering requests for songs. But better than that were the times when we children squatted in a circle, breathing in the musty smell of earth as we swapped ghost stories. Billy Bob would whisper that his grandma vowed that someday thunder would tear open the graves, and the dead would rise up.

But it never did. And when one of the men would finally ease open the door, allow that it was blowin' over, we children would run out, catch the warm raindrops on our tongues, and the fearful tales would be forgotten for a while.

Then it was that Friday late in March.

School was out that week for it was the time of plowing and farm children were needed in the fields. Mother was catching up on paper work, and Polly and I were allowed to play across the field in the sand ditch. But by midafternoon we had tired of building sand castles and decided to go to the schoolyard where we could have the seesaw all to ourselves.

I was facing toward the east as I bobbed up and down on the wooden plank. I could see the creek glistening gold with sunshine, the oak trees making lace patterns across the roof of our house.

Suddenly, as Polly's side rose high into the air, she cried out. "Look! Look behind you!" She was pointing toward the church spire, and then as her side went down again, she leaped from the seesaw so quickly I had to stiffen my legs to keep the plank from dropping to the ground.

I let go the handle and turned to look.

The monstrous cloud was boiling up from the

west. Its dark insides quivered with lightning. The edge of the cloud was hanging in shreds, like black voile ripped at the hem. Suddenly, the birds were stilled, the trees paralyzed, as if the breath had been sucked from the hills. There was no sign of life moving, no sound of plowing in the distance.

I gasped. "Run! Run!"

But Polly was already running. Her feet were splaying out behind her thin legs, her braids whipping her shoulders, faster, faster.

I went running behind her, racing toward the side yard where Mother was chasing after the baby chickens. "It's a storm!" I cried. "It's coming!"

But she was trying to shoo the chickens back into their wooden crate, and she didn't look up. "Help me get up the chickens," she said, " 'fore it rains."

Those chickens had been brought to us a few weeks ago by Mister Pope. He'd brought them the same day that he carried Rufus away.

Early that spring, our turkey's eyes had begun to droop, his feet became pale and crusted, his feathers began molting. Mother had asked Miz Pope to come take a look at him, and she'd come, taken one look, and then gone home to get The Mister to bring down the wagon. She'd quieted Polly and me by saying that she'd have to take Rufus up to her place to doctor him for a spell. So we hadn't cried much, for we were distracted by the baby chickens. But the next day she'd returned, said Rufus was old and ailing and that he'd passed on. "But now you have those pretty little chickens to take his place," she said. But she was wrong.

Those chickens were just fragile yellow fluffs we kept housed in the wooden crate with wire across the top. The crate was set on the sunny side of the porch where it was warm during the day, and Mother covered it with an old blanket at night. Polly and I fed them mash, and sometimes we reached in and touched the soft feathers beginning to form on their backs. But you couldn't tell one from the other, and so we didn't attempt to name them. Right from the start, Mother said that the chickens would be ready for the table this summer, that they'd be a big help to her during the months she received no pay from the county, so we didn't try to make pets of them. We just kept them fed and watered, and we put them out to scratch around the side yard while we aired out the crate.

Now the chickens were flitting in every direction, paying no mind as Mother called, "Here chick . . . chick . . . here chick . . ."

"The storm's comin'!" I gestured wildly. "The storm . . ."

Mother glanced up then, looking toward the west. At that moment, the cloud shrouded the sun, casting a greenish glow over the whole world. Mother put her hand to her forehead. "Oh, it . . . it is . . ." But the rest of her words were drowned out by the rushing river of wind. The trees began swaying, moaning, like something in the presence of death.

I ran to Mother, pulling at her skirt. "Let's run to the Piersons'!" I cried. "Run . . ."

"There's not time . . . it's coming too fast." She stooped down, grabbed a chicken, held it in the fold of her apron. "Help me get up the chickens 'fore they drown."

I saw that Polly was scrambling after the chickens too, already clutching one in her skirt. But the wind was whipping my hair across my face. Thunder was shaking the earth beneath my feet. Then I saw a flash of lightning strike the flagpole yonder in the schoolyard. A ball of fire rolled across the dirt.

Suddenly, I was running across the open field, heading for the shortcut that led up to the Piersons'. The wind was hard at my back, shoving me, making me stumble across the turned furrows. And then something grabbed my skirt. I screamed.

It was Mother. "Stop it, Mildred!" She was holding the back of my dress. "Get back to the house!"

She grabbed my hand, pulling me against the wind. Rain was hard as pebbles thrown into our faces. Our wet clothes clung to our legs, holding us back, as we struggled into the wind. Finally we ran up the slick wooden steps, stumbled across the wet porch while Polly held the door open.

Now the monstrous cloud was shaking the house, rattling the windows. I put my hands flat against the door, trying to hold it closed until Mother could get the straight chair, push it under the knob.

But she didn't run for the chair. She pulled me away from the door, opened it wide. "Wind's coming from the west," she said. "East door . . . I think . . . yes, east door should be open."

All the things I'd heard about storms came roaring back through my head. Lightning would strike us down. Thunder would open the graves. Wind would blow us all to Kingdom Come.

Mother was rushing through the house, setting pans under the leaks. Polly was wailing. "Our chickens are drownin'!" she cried. "I s-see 'em drowning!"

But I could only stand paralyzed with fear, sick with shame. I knew we'd have saved some of those chickens if I hadn't run. And now they were left to die because of me. This was Judgment Day, and I was doomed.

I ran into the bedroom, crawled beneath the bed. I lay there wet and shivering against the cold linoleum while the floor trembled and flashes of lightning reflected against the brass bedstead. Nothing could save me now. Perhaps no one in Willow Creek would be saved except the Piersons. The storm must've come up so fast that only they had time to get into the storm cellar, and when they finally emerged from that dark hole in the hill, there'd be only Billy Bob and his grandpa to hear Mrs. Pierson say, "The Lord surely intended . . ."

But now it was Mother I heard saying, "Come out from there!"

I opened my eyes and saw her stooping beneath the bedstead, looking under at me. I lay flat on my stomach, pressed my face against the floor till my nose ached. But Mother had grasped my ankles, and now I was sliding back across the wet linoleum, being pulled out from under the bed.

"Come out from there!" Mother drew me up on my feet. "You have to watch for falling trees."

Polly was standing there, too, and now Mother gave us instructions. "We'll stand inside the house long as we can. But if a big tree starts to fall, we've got to be ready to run."

She motioned me toward the kitchen. "Take your post beneath that window. Keep low, but keep watching that oak." Polly was to watch out the east window, and Mother the west.

"Now, if a tree looks as if it'll fall," she said, "holler loud as you can. Otherwise," she said firmly, "no crying!"

But now we were standing in the middle room where the door was ajar. Already, the rain was sweeping across the porch as if the raging storm were on the threshold, ready to pounce inside.

"But I can't!" I cried. "I can't!" I tightened my eyes. "I don't like to watch!"

Mother was marching me on into the kitchen, pushing me down beneath the window. "You don't have to like it," she said. "You have to *do* it!"

And so I did. For what seemed an eternity, I knelt there in the dark kitchen, hearing the rain leaking into the enamel pan, the thunder rattling the windows. I saw lightning streaking through the sky, trees writhing in the wind. I watched leaves torn from branches, branches torn from trees. Several times, the oak swayed toward our roof as if it would crash down upon us, but just as I'd open my mouth to cry out, the tree would right itself, and I'd gulp back the scream in my throat.

Gradually, I became aware that the thunder was rumbling off toward the east, like a distant train. The wind was easing, the rain settling into a drizzle. Slowly, I pulled myself up, leaned against the windowsill, and looked out into the side yard.

The yard was strewn with leaves and twigs, as if the trees had undressed there in the yard. And yet the fallen branches had formed leafy shelters for the chickens, shielding them from the downpour. Now I saw a leaf move. One chicken was shaking its wet, thin wings.

I ran out the back door through the drizzling rain. I picked up the chicken, feeling its fragile bones beneath the wet feathers, the faint pulsing from its heart. I shouted out to Mother. "The chickens are alive! They're alive!"

They were not all alive, but after we'd searched among the branches, turned over the leaves, we found eight that showed some signs of life. We carried them into the kitchen. Mother spread a towel over the biscuit pan, laid the chickens on it, and placed them in the warming oven of the stove.

As we emptied rainwater from the pans and mopped up the floor, I kept running back to the warming oven, putting my ear against the iron door. Finally there was a faint "cheep . . . cheep." I eased open the door and peeked inside.

A little bedraggled creature stretched its neck and peeked back at me. Soon others were wobbling to their feet, pecking at their wings, and though some continued to lie cold and still, six of them revived.

By the time we'd changed into dry clothes, the trees were dappled with sunshine, the birds were out hopping over the wet grass.

We went to stand out on the porch, breathing in the cool fresh air. We heard the clanging of cowbells, like an all clear, as the animals went plodding over the hillsides, heading for the barns.

"Well, that's another storm we've weathered," Mother said. "That's one we looked right in the eye, and we weathered it."

I sighed. "I hope it's the last," I said. "I hope I never have to eye another one."

She pushed my hair back from my ears, fluffing up the dampness. "But you will, honey," she said softly. "You will. But you'll remember that you can. You'll remember that sometimes you have to."

Her words followed me, like a prophecy, through the years, through the times when I've stood in the path of the storm, facing something that must be done, no matter how frightening, how painful. *But you don't have to like it,* I hear her say. *You just have to do it.*

And then I turn to face the ill wind and, finally, to weather it through.

10

The year was ending, but winter still foraged over the Tennessee hills. It would be some time yet before the thin, gaunt trees were nourished by spring. So folks paid little heed to the coming of January. They prepared for it only by taking down the calendar that hung alongside the kitchen range, getting out the new one that'd arrived with the seed catalogue, and seeing to their supply of black-eyed peas.

Late in December, Miz Pope had come by just as she always did, bringing Mother the sack of dried peas, the hunk of hog jowl. "Now don't forget to soak the peas overnight," she said, "and then cook 'em up with the hog jowl. Be sure ya'll eat 'em on New Year's Day!" She smiled, wiping her fingers over the front of her apron.

Her plump body was always encased in an apron that bulged toward the middle, as if she'd taken the style as well as the material from flour sacks. "It'll bring you luck!" she said, just as she had every year since we'd come to Willow Creek.

The first year when she'd come bringing the peas, Mother had taken the sack, thanked her, and then smiling at Miz Pope she'd said, "But surely you don't believe ..."

But then she'd seen the way Miz Pope puffed up, frowning, and she'd said quickly, "Why, yes, of course ..." Because, of course, Miz Pope did.

Folks in these parts were always courting Lady Luck, using whatever charm they could muster. A rusted horseshoe was nailed over every barn door. The hind foot of a rabbit swung from a hook on every back porch. And bags of ripe-smelling asafetida were strung around the necks of every schoolchild to ward off germs.

When we'd first started to school in Willow Creek, Polly and I had not worn the asafetida like the other children. Mother said it was bad enough to have to smell it in the closed schoolrooms all winter long without having it permeating our house, too. But then, Mother used all her energies to deal with the realities of life, not the superstitions. She trusted in hard work and self-reliance to see her through the lean days, the long nights of caring for her children, of trying to make a home for us there in the hills.

But it happened that the first winter we were there, Polly and I both caught whooping cough the same week, and the only available remedy was a spoonful of coal oil mixed with sugar.

All that week Mother had run back and forth from

the schoolhouse, trying to get us to keep down some sassafras tea, some chicken broth. All through the night, she was up mixing the coal oil and sugar, holding a pan under our chins while we whooped. And so on Saturday morning when Miz Pope appeared at the door, bringing two small flannel sacks tied with crocheted cord and said, "I'd see to it the chillun wear these when they go back to school," Mother had nodded, too weary even to wrinkle her nose, and she saw to it.

The asafetida worked like a charm. It kept us out in the fresh air whenever there was a ray of sun, and we stayed reasonably healthy for the rest of the winter.

In time Polly and I learned from the other children to spit when we saw a caterpillar (else you get a fever), to walk around the same side of a tree (else you'll have a fuss), and now that we'd been here several years, we'd become practitioners in the art of wishing.

So it was that late in November of this year, we were walking across the field from school when I saw a new moon, pale in the afternoon sky. "Make a wish!" I cried, and then, "*I* wish to make a hundred in spelling!"

I had progressed to Mother's room now, leaving Polly behind with Miss Wilkins. But Mother went out of her way not to show me any partiality, and when she called on me to write a word on the blackboard, it was often the hardest word in the lesson. I rarely got to turn down anyone in spelling.

"Won't come true," Polly said. "You wished out loud."

"Will too," I insisted. "A new moon's lucky."

Mother stopped there in the frozen field and looked down at me. "You'll get a hundred when you've earned it," she said. "It takes more'n luck to accomplish anything. It takes work." And being accustomed to teaching, she followed with an example. "Why, would it help if I just wished for our supper and didn't work for it?"

I reached for her hand. It felt small inside the woolen glove. "I'll wish for you!" I said. And I did.

We walked on past the brittle cornstalks, stepped up onto our wooden porch. And there was a sack of sausage with a note from Miz Pope. "We kild hawgs today," it said.

Mother laughed out loud, and Polly said, "You didn't wish out loud, see?"

But after we'd eaten our supper of sausage and biscuits with sorghum, Mother said, "Now get out your books and work a little harder on your spelling tonight."

So during those November nights, we three sat at the oilcloth-covered table with Mother grading papers and Polly and me studying, and then Mother would hear our lessons.

Gradually I began to improve, even to turn down some of the children in my class. I didn't reach the head of the class, nor did I make a hundred, but I kept trying, and Mother said she was pleased with my progress. And though I accepted the fact that studying harder did help, I still put my hands behind my back and crossed my fingers when it came my turn to recite.

Once, when we were leaving the store, I found an Indian head penny there beside the road. I resisted the temptation to rush back and buy licorice. Secretly, I put it in my shoe and limped around on it until Mother discovered what I'd done and sighed that I'd surely taken up foolish notions.

But now, just before the new year, Miz Pope had brought us the black-eyed peas, the hog jowl, had reminded us again that eatin' 'em would bring us luck. And this time I believed it to be an omen. I'd been looking for something really special, some way of making my fondest wish come true. Maybe this was it.

On New Year's Day, after we were seated at the round table and Mother had said the blessing, I said, "Shouldn't we make a wish before we eat?"

Mother spooned the dark peas, the chunks of ham, onto my plate and passed me the hot cornbread. "We're eating the peas because they're nourishing," she said. "But you may make a New Year's resolution."

"Out loud?" I said.

She nodded.

164

Perhaps I should've just made my wish and kept it secret. But I'd been cuddling one wonderful dream for weeks now, waiting for just the right time, just the right lucky charm to put with it. And I wanted desperately to believe Miz Pope.

"I wish . . ." I began.

"I resolve . . ." she corrected me.

"I resolve," I said, taking a deep breath, "to win the spelling bee over the whole school!"

Then I heaped a spoonful of peas, a piece of ham, onto my cornbread and popped it into my mouth.

The spelling bee was scheduled for the end of February.

It would be held in the Community Church, and promised to be the most exciting happening since last fall when the visiting preacher had baptized five people in the creek. The contest was to be conducted throughout the school system in the entire county, with the winner from each grade being sent to Town for the finals.

Our school was so small it could send only one pupil, but a system of rating had been devised to select the best speller from his particular age group, and then he or she would represent the community of Willow Creek.

This, in itself, was a coveted honor. But even more than that, to me, was the fact that the contestant's mother would get to go, too. A bus would come through the surrounding hills, picking up the lucky ones, and then they'd all go riding to Town. They'd be put up, in grand style, at a boardinghouse, and even go in a group to the picture show before returning.

I hadn't yet figured how to get Polly included, too, but I'd wish on that later. For now, my wish was that it'd be Mother's student, not Miss Wilkins', who was judged best in the school. And it would be Mother who got to wear her good blue dress and mingle with the fancy folks. I could just see her, all gay and smiling, being proud of her work as a teacher, of her daughter who could spell better'n anyone in Willow Creek.

Now Mother was looking at the way I was chewing with my mouth full. "You've bitten off quite a lot there," she said.

But I just nodded, swallowed the cornbread. I wiped my mouth with the napkin before I said, "What's your resolution, Polly?"

Polly had already begun eating. "Oh . . . I dunno . . ."

Actually, Polly didn't need black-eyed peas to bring her luck. She was a blue-eyed, blonde child with dark, thick lashes. Recently, she'd begged until Mother cut her braids, and now her hair hung light and fluffy around her small ears. The boys were always writing her notes, bringing her fragrant buds of Sweet Betsy to tie in the corner of her handkerchief. Miss Wilkins was always bragging on her arithmetic, telling Mother that Polly could add faster than any student she'd ever taught. And though her spelling grades were only fair, Miss Wilkins said Polly shouldn't worry her pretty head about that, it'd come in time. So if wishes were horses, Polly's were easily saddled.

"Why don't you resolve," Mother said to her now, "to brush your hair every night? One hundred strokes."

Polly nodded. "All right."

"And I'll resolve," Mother said softly, tracing the pattern of oilcloth with her finger, "I'll resolve to be thankful for the fruition of each day, to make our lives rich and full."

And so we began the New Year.

A fresh snow fell in January, and Mother said she was thankful that we'd gone into the woods during Christmas vacation and gathered armloads of pine kindling. Polly sat by the blazing fire, her hair crackling with electricity as she brushed and counted, practicing her arithmetic with each stroke. And I worked on spelling 'til I could still see the letters after I was in bed with my eyes closed.

We began the new year as people always do, with firm determination that our resolutions be kept.

But as January was torn from the calendar and the February sleigh-scene appeared, we began to slip a little.

Mother developed a chest cold, and the walk home from school left her chilled and coughing. At night, as she sat at the table grading papers, she'd lean her head on her hand, saying little.

Polly was starting division now, and she would divide out loud, losing count of the number of brushstrokes.

I had begun to lag behind in geography, and Mother said that I must bone up on the state capitals and not put all my time on spelling.

Then it was two weeks before the date set for the spelling bee. I was sitting at the table studying while Mother was fixing supper. I looked up across the lamplight. "Mother," I said, "I won't win." I sighed. "Even if I win in my grade, I can't beat the whole school."

She was standing at the stove, stirring the pot with a wooden spoon. Tonight she was heating up some black-eyed peas, making some cornbread. Maybe it was because there was little else, or maybe she felt that we all needed a reminder. "You resolved to try," she said. "Remember?"

"Yes'm," I sighed, and began again. I crammed my head with letters, words, phrases to help me remember—"i before e . . . except after c . . . and sometimes y . . ."

But I also remembered to watch out for any black cat that might cross my path, and often I crossed my fingers so hard the knuckles ached. One day at school I saw that Billy Bob Pierson had a four-leaf clover pressed between the pages of his speller. I offered him a box of yellow pencils, which Uncle Marvin had sent me for Christmas, if he'd trade spellers with me. I might have gotten the book for less, because Billy Bob had said he hadn't the least notion of trying out for the spelling bee. But though his book was smudged and held together with flour paste, the four-leaf clover had put a visible sign of luck on the pages, and I needed all the help I could get.

As the day approached when Mother would announce the top students from each class, I begged her to tell me if I had a chance. But she only said that I must keep working. Then the day came, and I saw she was trying to hold back a smile as she picked up the chalk and turned to the blackboard. She wrote the classes, the points made, the names of the winners. And I was among them. I'd been given a chance!

On Saturday morning the District Superintendent came out from Town, and all the folks in Willow Creek gathered at the church.

Emily and Chet Daniels were there with little Emilene all gussied up in a crocheted coat and bonnet which Miz Wilson, like a doting grandmother, had made for her.

Wade Sanders and Isabel were there with their first born, a boy whose name was McFarland Sanders, but everybody called him Mac.

Out in the vestibule, Mister Pope was lifting planks onto the saw-horses, readying the tables, while Miz Pope supervised where the women should

set their platters of baked ham and stuffed eggs
and their chess pies.

I saw that Mother was standing over to the side,
talking with the Superintendent. Polly was looking
at a flint arrow which one of the boys had brought
her. I slipped over to Miz Pope, tugged at her apron.

"Wish me luck, Miz Pope," I whispered.

She wiped her hands. She patted my head. "Oh I
do, child," she said. "I most rightly do!"

There were eight of us who lined up in front of
the chancel, folded our hands, and breathlessly faced
the Superintendent. He started with the first-grade
pupil, giving him a simple word. When he got to me,
he said "rabbit," and fortunately I remembered about
the two "b's." The first round was over now, and I
was still standing.

I looked out into the pews and saw that Mother
was smiling. So was Miz Pope.

But now the words began to get harder, and on the
second round, I got the "i" and "e" turned around.
But you were allowed to miss once before you were
disqualified, so I continued to stand there, my palms
sweating, my mouth drying up, as the other pupils
took their turns. The second round was over.

Then, on the third round, the Superintendent
looked at his list, looked at me, and said, "balloon."

"B-a-l . . ." I began, and then remembering that it
had two "o's," I said "B-a-l-o-o-n!"

He shook his head.

A murmur drifted up from the audience.

He said, "You may sit down."

He said it twice before I could make my legs move, before I could cross there in front of everybody and sit down on the front bench. My chin was trembling, but I kept blinking fast, determined not to cry, not to disgrace Mother any worse than I had. I kept my face to the front as I slid down the bench, making room as one by one the other losers came to join me. And finally the freckled girl from Miss Wilkins' third grade stood alone and triumphant.

I ached for it to be over now, so I could run out behind the tombstones and hide my face and cry.

But even after the winner was declared, the Superintendent wouldn't release the losers. He called for us to come line up in front of the chancel again, and announced that we'd have what he called "consolation." He presented each of us with a heavy volume, bound in smooth leather, with notches in the gold-edged pages. "An encyclopedia," he said.

If this was consolation, it was, to me, no better than charity. But I was able to murmur "thank you" while I kept my eyes lowered, bit my lip, until we were finally dismissed from the eyes of the congregation.

Folks were starting to mill around now, lining up for the church dinner. I started for the side door. But Mother was pushing her way through the crowd, coming up to me.

"You did just fine," she said, patting my arm. "It's all right now . . . it's all right . . ."

But it wasn't all right. I ached with all the pain of childhood, of wishing I could make my mother happy, of being so helpless against all that had happened. I kept my head down, trying to hold back tears.

I didn't notice that Miz Pope had come up to me, too, until I saw her fingers stroking the leather book.

"Now aren't you a lucky girl!" she said. "Such a pretty book, all your own."

I couldn't answer her. I kept shaking my head, not looking at her, until Mother said, "She'll feel better after she has something to eat."

But though she got a plate for me, heaped it with all my favorites—country ham and pickled peaches and corn pudding—my throat hurt too much to try to eat. Even when Billy Bob ran over and said, "Hey, Mil, look! The outside piece of Grandma's chocolate cake!" I just shook my head and told him I wasn't hungry.

Finally, folks began leaving. Mother and Polly and I were pulling on our coats when Miz Pope called us aside. "There's lots of chicken left," she said. "Y'all take it for your supper." She handed Mother a plate covered with a clean dishcloth.

As we started down the road toward home, I said, "I'm not going to eat any of Miz Pope's chicken. Not any of her ole black-eyed peas either. Not ever again!"

"Hush now," Mother said. "That isn't nice."

But I was feeling sorry for myself, feeling angry and betrayed. "I don't care," I said. "She told a lie!"

"Hush now," Mother said.

But I kept getting angrier and angrier as we walked on up the path and went into the somber old house. Now Polly was taking off her wool cap, fluffing out her hair, and Mother was laying the fire just as if nothing had happened, just as if the world had not come to an end.

Finally I blurted out, "*You* told a lie, too!"

Mother turned and stared, open-mouthed, at me.

"Miz Pope said I should make a wish," I said. "And *you* said I should make a resolution. And I did ... and ... and ..." And suddenly my body was shaking, wracked with the sobs I'd held tight inside me.

Mother knelt down beside me, put her arms around my waist. After a moment she said, "But, honey, resolutions do help. Even if they're kept for only a little while, they do help."

"They don't," I sobbed. "They don't!"

Mother moved back to the rocker then, drawing me into her lap. My legs were long and thin as a colt's now, and I was too big, too gangling, to be rocked like a baby. And yet, just once more, I allowed myself the solace of leaning my head back against her shoulder, of letting the tears flow while she patted my knee, rocked me back and forth.

"You know," she said softly, "I was just wondering. . . . I was just wondering if maybe we were both right. Miz Pope and I. Maybe luck *is* where you find it, once you've resolved to dig for it."

The room was growing warm now, and Mother slowed the rocker, gently pushed me up out of her lap.

She walked over to the table, picked up the leather-bound book. "Aren't we fortunate to have such a beautiful book?" she said. "Let's see what wonderful things we might find in it."

So that night, and during the many nights and days to come, she read to us from the encyclopedia, beginning with Aaron, brother of Moses, who made the golden calf. She made each topic an adventure, reading first the facts and then encouraging us to use the magic carpet of our imaginations. And so, though we lived in the lean, hushed hills, we were also in Holland wearing wooden shoes. Sometimes, we landed with the Pilgrims and considered ways of making friends with the Indians. And once, when the snow veiled our windows, we rode off to Zanzibar with the Sultan. We returned, at our leisure, to the gold-edged book.

The book became scuffed and torn through the years, but still I kept it, moving it with me from place to place, through years that brought laughter or loneliness. But gradually I forgot about it, shelving it for a newer volume.

It was by chance that I was reminded of it again this year, late in December.

I'd gone to the shopping center where the magic of Christmas was being elbowed out by the year-end sales. The snow was only a gray slush, cast off in the gutters now. The bell ringers were gone from the corner, leaving it to the rack of newspapers with their chilling headlines.

With a vague sense of depression, I went on into the supermarket, began pushing my cart down the aisle. It was then I chanced to see a sack of black-eyed peas.

They were in modern dress now, but they looked out at me through the cellophane like long-forgotten friends.

I stood for a moment, smiling, remembering.

Then I lifted them into my cart, took them home with me. I took down the old encyclopedia, dusted off the gold edges, set it here between the bookends.

Soon now, it will be time to put the peas to soak.